Praise for Jeanne M. Dams
and **The Body in the Transept**

The Body in the Transept

A DOROTHY MARTIN MYSTERY

Jeanne M. Dams

HarperPaperbacks
A Division of HarperCollinsPublishers

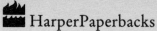 HarperPaperbacks
A Division of HarperCollins*Publishers*
10 East 53rd Street, New York, N.Y. 10022-5299

 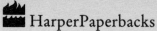

To two wonderful men:
My father, Lawrence Martin,
and my husband, Ed, who always believed in me.

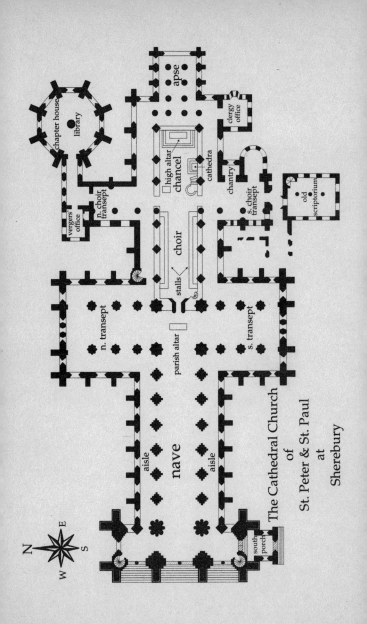

The Cathedral Church of St. Peter & St. Paul at Sherebury

The Body
in the
Transept

A DOROTHY MARTIN MYSTERY

⚘ 1 ⚘

I WAS STRUGGLING against more than wind and rain that night as I battled through the Cathedral Close, but I blamed my mood on the weather. This was *not* my idea of a proper English Christmas. The air ought to shiver in a frosty stillness broken only by church bells chiming with the peculiar clarity of sound carried on intensely cold air. The sweet piping of young carolers should catch at the throat. My mind's eye costumed the carolers in crinolines and fur muffs, greatcoats and stovepipe hats, and set them beside a gas streetlamp, gently falling snow sparkling in the soft amber light. . . .

As I wandered happily in my nineteenth-century fantasy, I slipped on a wet, irregular paving stone and was rudely returned to reality. There were bells, to be sure, pealing away in cheerful discord. But the path was lit (more or less) by electricity, faint diesel fumes perfumed the air, and neat black-and-white plastic signs pointed my way. Not even the great medieval cathedral, looming out of the stinging rain, could transcend the twentieth century entirely; she wore an ugly modern veil of scaffolding over part of her ancient, crumbling face.

By exercising great care I reached the door to the south porch without turning an ankle or, more important, ruining my new hat. The thought of my Christmas hat cheered me considerably. It was a silly thing, really, a confection in bright green with red plastic holly berries dangling from a drift of white net, but I loved it. What did I care if it was entirely unsuitable for a woman my age? As I shook out my umbrella one of the berries detached itself and dropped wetly down my neck; it took a shake like a sheepdog's to dislodge it.

In keeping with time-honored English tradition the porch was at least as cold as the night outside, but it was reasonably dry. I jammed the umbrella into a tightly packed stand and hung up my coat, now soaking wet and useless. My tweed suit might be warm enough to keep me from freezing in the church. Hat resettled and glasses straightened, I moved into the nave.

The sight that greeted me lowered my spirits again. Sherebury Cathedral boasts one of the longest naves in England, indeed in the world, several hundred feet of glory from great west door to choir screen, with seating for thousands. Yet the flickering light from the candles in the huge chandeliers showed me only a few empty chairs at the very back. I was flabbergasted. The English, as this century staggers toward its death, don't share the convictions of the people of the Age of Faith who built the huge churches; the usual congregation at Sherebury fits nicely into the choir. Tonight, though, it seemed that half England had braved the weather to see Christmas in. Where in heaven's name was I to find a seat?

At least all those people made it almost warm, but I was wet and tired and my feet hurt. When a person is sixty-something and weighs more than she ought, she doesn't relish the prospect of standing through a long, late church service in festive shoes. I looked around vaguely for a verger, but they all seemed to be down near the choir screen in some sort of powwow, gesturing and arguing and paying not the slightest attention to their duties. Very well, I'd have to fend for myself.

I hoped I wouldn't have to settle for one of those chairs at the back, where I wouldn't see a thing. Sherebury's choir screen is a masterpiece, the pinnacle of the stone-carver's art, but I hadn't planned to spend the whole evening staring at it and getting a draft on the back of my neck in the bargain. Furthermore, the scaffolding up against one side of the screen disfigured the whole nave. Restoration is necessary, but I didn't want to look at it on Christmas Eve.

There was no point in just standing there; I sighed and began to look around for a small miracle. There might be someone I knew in all that crowd, with maybe an empty seat?

The trouble was, it wasn't like an American church with pews. You can almost always squeeze one more into a pew if you're willing to risk a few glares. Chairs are a different matter.

As I moved up the center of the nave I searched for familiar faces. I'd been in Sherebury long enough to know a number of people, at least casually. That's one of the beauties of the town. It's small, as cathedral towns go, and as in any small English town even today most of the residents know each other. An incoming American is enough of a curiosity to be noticed.

On the whole I had been treated well enough. People I knew from earlier visits had been kind and introduced me to their friends, and I'd been invited to tea and drinks. They didn't know quite what to do with me, though. I didn't fit into any of their patterns, circles revolving around the cathedral, or the university, or the families who had lived there time out of mind. That was perhaps why no one had invited me to come with them to mid-night Mass. Then, too, Christmas tends to be a family affair, while I . . . ah! There was Jane.

My next-door neighbor, Jane Langland, is my only
real friend in Sherebury. It's easy to dismiss Jane as just a
typical English spinster. She looks and sounds a good
deal like Winston Churchill, and dispenses gallons of tea
and oceans of gruff sympathy. It took me a while to dis-
cover that Jane is typical of no one but herself. Behind the
brusque facade is a mind of diamond—and a heart of
custard.

An extremely competent teacher recently retired from
a local school, she knows every child in town. I wasn't
surprised to find her sitting composedly in the midst of a
crowd of giggling teenagers. Former students, except perhaps for one dark boy who drew attention to himself by
his stillness. His blue jeans were frayed and much too
tight, his shirt thin and worn. He looked older than the
others, whom he ignored as he slouched in his chair, chin
hunched into his chest, arms hugged in tightly. It
occurred to me that the defiant posture might be due as
much to cold as to bad manners. Evidently the same
thought came to Jane, for she passed over her own tweed
jacket. I was mildly surprised to see the young man take it
and drape it over his thin shoulders, his blue eyes flashing a glance of thanks.

Jane looked up and saw me then. I couldn't hear her
over the noisy kids, but the waves and shrugs said clearly
enough that she'd be delighted to have me join them but
she didn't see where one extra person could be put. I gestured my thanks and understanding, and moved on.

There was a seat! Alice Chambers seemed to be alone
with an empty chair beside her, on the aisle, too, where I
could see the procession, and close enough to the choir
screen to afford me at least a glimpse of the activity at the
altar. Alice was looking very attractive, dressed impecca-
bly in soft blue wool, hair and nails lacquered to perfection, so she might be expecting someone. But then Alice
always manages to look like that. I've long cherished a

secret notion that she wears her pearls in the bath. More the dumpling type myself, I'm consumed with envy of Alice's effortless elegance.

I wouldn't have chosen her as a companion for the evening; she's always intimidated me. But my shoes were pinching and my options were limited.

"Merry Christmas, Alice!" My cheery greeting sounded put on, even to me. "Are you saving this seat for someone?"

"Oh, Dorothy! Merry Christmas! Sorry, it's for my husband, if he ever turns up." Alice allowed a tinge of exasperation to color her well-modulated voice. "George is late, as usual. He promised me quite faithfully he'd be here by ten-thirty on the dot so we could sit in the choir, and here it is after eleven and he's vanished. You've not seen him, have you?"

"No, I just got here myself." I sagged back to normal and tried to swallow my disappointment. "Stupid of me to be so late, but I didn't realize—I mean it's been years since I was here for Christmas Eve, and usually the place is half empty . . ."

"Oh, dear, and here I am with an extra chair. I'm so sorry, I would offer it to you, but he *said* he would be here . . ."

"And here he is, isn't he?" The genial voice came from behind us. "So sorry, my dear, got held up at my office. You knew I'd turn up sooner or later. *Good* evening, Dorothy, you're looking blooming."

So was George, and from the aroma wafting my way, his bloom was artificially induced; he wasn't usually so cordial to me. I wondered which pub George had holed up in while Alice fretted. Since when did the university have office hours on Christmas Eve? Well, best tend to my own business and leave them to have it out. "Thank you, George. Nice to see you both. Excuse me, I think I'm going to see if there's any room in the choir."

I hurried through the arch and scanned the stalls on either side of the aisle, beginning to get really anxious. This was the prime spot, of course, and would have filled up long ago, but there might be a chance, someone else who was late, or had changed his mind . . .

A verger materialized next to me, talking while squinting up in outrage at the gorgeous brass chandelier, one of whose candles was dripping. "I'm sorry, madam, the h'empty stalls are reserved for the choir and clergy."

"Yes, I know." My voice was acid enough to attract his condescending attention.

"Oh, h'it's you, Mrs. Martin." There wasn't a lot of Christmas cheer in his manner, either.

"Good evening, Mr. Wallingford. I know it's hopeless, but I thought I might find a place to stand."

"Oh, but we can't 'ave standing in the choir on Christmas Eve, can we—too many candles h'about, we 'as to keep the h'exits clear. Danger of fire, you know." He sounded quite pleased about it, and I gritted my teeth. This was petty English officialdom at its worst, someone whose function was to serve the public taking delight in snubbing them instead.

"Well then, don't bother about me, I'll manage." I swept away in a burst of temper I regretted before I had taken two steps. The odious man might have helped if I'd played on his sense of chivalry instead of getting indignant. Assuming he had a sense of chivalry. As it was, those back rows of the nave were looking better all the time.

One last despairing glance at the choir stalls before I turned to leave—and my small miracle happened. I saw an empty stall, and actually in the second row!

"Excuse me, is someone sitting there?" It couldn't happen, could it? They would have gone to the bathroom, or to fetch a program, or . . .

"Not as I know of. Me wife got sleepy and went 'ome.

Dunno as you'll fit." The fat man in the next stall looked appraisingly at my own well-nourished contours; I felt a little like one of the farm animals I would bet were his daily companions. He was obviously displeased at the idea of a neighbor, but I was past caring. The seat was right in the middle of the row, so I pardoned and excused and squeezed my way past the knees and the hassocks and a few glares, smiled graciously at the fat man (which annoyed him still further), and slipped to my knees with a sigh of relief. So annoying to be late, but how lucky to have found a place at all, and it was only because I was alone. Most people wanted two seats together.

And at the thought, with no warning, depression possessed me utterly. It was like that. It always struck unexpectedly, when I had forgotten, before I could put up my defenses. It would lie in wait for a chance to remind me that I was—alone. That only a year ago I had been celebrating Christmas with Frank, vigorous, apparently healthy Frank, looking forward to retirement in June, the two of us planning our move to the England we adored. This should have been a moment to enjoy together, our first Christmas in our new home. Instead I was congratulating myself on finding a single seat. A widow's seat.

I squeezed my eyes tight shut, but too late. A tear worked its way out and rolled down my cheek, and the more I tried to will the demon away, the more insistent became its jabs. I *knew* force never worked against it. Anyway, what was the good of resisting? All the courage in the world wouldn't change anything. I was alone. What an idiot I'd been to think about leaving familiar surroundings for a place where everyone tried to be kind, but no one really understood. No one spoke my language. Oh, I had plenty of acquaintances, but they had a different sense of humor, different ways of doing things. I'd never be one of them.

As the tide of self-pity rose to drown any other

thought, any hope of comfort, I stopped trying to say my prayers. There was plainly no point. No, I would sit there and wallow in misery. Despising myself, and adding despicableness to the roster of my woes, I creaked back into the hard, upright seat, sniffed, and raised my chin in martyrly fashion.

And the cathedral took over. Far above my head it soared—the cathedral by candlelight. An unimaginable weight of flame-gilded stone, defying gravity, rushed skyward and spread, lacelike, into the miracle of England's finest fan-vaulted choir. Rank on rank of wood and stone saints and kings and apostles looked down on me from choir stalls and niches, carved draperies swaying a little, features shaping into half-smiles or reproving frowns with the flicker of candles far below. Five centuries of worship, seeping from ancient stones, embraced me in the warm arms of faith and tradition. The heady scents of incense and evergreen, the subdued, exciting bustle of voices, light and color and movement, all spoke of something to come, something cosmic and magnificent.

Awestruck, senses sated and numbed with beauty, I forgot to be unhappy. I was even able to grin at myself as I mopped away the silly tears. The demon wouldn't appreciate being overcome by architecture, but it didn't stand a chance here, not for long. I couldn't be miserable even when I tried, not on Christmas Eve in the most beautiful church in the world.

"I beg your pardon." The voice at my elbow sounded apologetic. I had an uncomfortable feeling that this diffident man in tweeds had been trying to get my attention for some time. "Sorry to bother you, but I believe we're meant to take one of these." He held out a box full of slender candles and small cardboard circles, carefully not looking at me.

Oh, dear. He'd seen me crying. I felt a blush rising, but I couldn't very well explain myself to a total stranger. "Of course," I murmured, not looking at him, either. "Thank you." I took a candle and drip-catcher from the box and passed it along to the fat man, who grunted.

As I slid the disk onto the bottom of my candle, I chanced a sideways glance at the man in tweeds. He was a big man, not flabby like my fat neighbor on the other side, but tall and substantial, with lots of soft, wavy gray hair. As my look slid up to his kind but firm-looking face, my eye caught his and I looked away in embarrassment.

"I do beg your pardon, but are you by any chance Mrs. Martin?" His solid, comfortable voice sounded just the way his face looked.

I turned back to him and stared. Aside from a strong resemblance to Alistair Cooke, his features were completely unfamiliar. I was sure I'd never seen him before. "Why yes, I am, but . . ."

He smiled. "No, it isn't second sight. I know your neighbor, Jane Langland, and she's mentioned you to me. Especially your—er—taste in hats. I quite like this one, if I may say so." The smile broadened slightly, although he was much too polite to let it turn into a chuckle.

I relaxed and laughed. "I know it's an extremely silly one—but thank you very much, I like it too, Mr.—?"

"Nesbitt. Alan Nesbitt." He shook my hand.

"And how do you know Jane?" I was genuinely curious. Jane's orbit did not, as far as I knew, include many distinguished-looking men, except for the cathedral staff, and I knew most of them by sight.

"I met her on official business a year or so ago."

I looked blank.

"Sorry, I should have explained I'm chief constable for this county. Miss Langland's house was burgled last year, and she came to me in great distress, convinced we had the wrong man. She was quite right, in fact. She gave me no peace until we caught the real villain."

I laughed. "I can imagine. Jane's almost always right

about people, and she's a tiger for justice." I laughed again at the thought of Jane as a tiger—a plump, gray-haired, very English tiger—and was about to voice the image when the great organ over our heads uttered a mighty chord that made human speech inaudible. I shrugged and smiled. A mellow light began to spread through the choir as the vergers lit a few congregational candles and each passed on the gentle flame. The last electric lights were turned out; the sonorous fugue rolled over us and we settled back in satisfaction. Bach, I thought dreamily. Perfect for Christmas. The great ritual was beginning.

The service proceeded in its familiar order, with extra flourishes for Christmas. Sherebury is "high-church"—very Catholic in its practices—so clouds of incense led in the cathedral clergy in their glistening white-and-gold vestments. Vergers headed the procession in the red and blue and green cassocks of their rank, stained-glass colors that were their usual garb but looked specially chosen for the festive season. The dean followed the canons, wearing his tall dignity with a benign humility. The bishop, a small man made majestic in embroidered cope and mitre, brought up the rear, carrying his deeply carved silver crozier. And all the while the choirboys in ruffled surplices and the men in more tailored versions sang like the very archangels.

The bishop ascended his throne, the "cathedra" for which the building was named. Not being especially fond of the bishop, I confess to the irreverent thought that he looked far too insignificant for the splendor of that chair. Carved of oak and nestled in a hooded niche of miraculously lacy marble that stretched upward for twenty feet or more, it seemed more fitting for the real Owner of the building. Everyone else took their appointed places for the stately choreography of a high-church service, and the dean began the measured poetry of Archbishop Cranmer.

"Almighty God, unto whom all hearts be open, all desires known. . . ."

As the service wore on, the vast congregation of strangers seemed to unite in the mood of that night of miracles, joining lustily in the hymns and carols. They gave us all the old favorites: "Away in a Manger," "Hark, the Herald Angels Sing," "What Child Is This." I did my enthusiastic best until they came to "O Little Town of Bethlehem." Then the pure beauty of the boy soprano's descant put such a lump in my throat that I couldn't sing a note. No matter that I know perfectly well they're normal mischievous little boys, not angels straight from heaven; when they sing in that particular way I melt to a puddle.

The sermon was brief and cheering, the communion solemnly moving. As I made my way back from the altar rail I reveled in the exalted sense of goodwill that one always hopes will last. It never does, of course. In a while I would remember my troubles. I would begin to let the little worries nag at me, and be annoyed by the fat man's wheezes and elbowings. I would come down to earth. But even knowing that, for just one sublime suspended moment nothing could spoil the perfection of Christmas, the first Christmas and this one somehow joined as one.

It was long after midnight, truly Christmas, when the slender congregational candles flickered their last, the bishop pronounced the benediction, and the organ broke into a final delighted riot of sound. I sat while the others began to leave, well content to let the glory flow over me until the last triumphant chord rolled away and was swallowed up in the greetings of "Merry Christmas" sounding from all sides. I heaved a huge sigh of satisfaction and rose, a trifle creakily, from the confinement of my narrow stall. A courteous hand at my elbow reminded me of Mr. Nesbitt's presence.

"Thank you. I think I'm getting too old for late hours

and hard seats. Lovely as that was, I'm stiff and tired and ready for home."

"I'd be delighted to see you home, Mrs. Martin. Unless you have other friends here . . ."

"No, I was planning on going home alone. It's very kind of you, but you don't need to bother, I'll be fine. It's only a few steps, just the other side of the Close."

"No bother at all. I believe the cloister door would be the nearest, wouldn't it?" He steered me away from the crowd going out through the nave. He was quite right. It was quite a walk through the Close to my house from the south door, while the cloister door led directly to the little gate into my street.

"Goodness, it's dark!" I stumbled over a paving stone in the south choir transept, grateful once again for the steadying hand. "I suppose they left these lights off for effect."

"Actually I believe it's something to do with the rewiring. Did you have a coat, Mrs. Martin? It's quite chilly."

I stopped in dismay. "Oh, dear. It's in the south porch. My umbrella, too. I came in that way because this door was locked from the outside. Maybe we should go out the front after all."

"No, no, we'll be able to get *out*, I'm sure. I'll just go and fetch your things for you, if you'll tell me what color . . ."

"A new Burberry, with a red scarf in the pocket. And the umbrella has cats all over it, in bright colors."

Again I caught that suggestion of a chuckle as he turned away.

"I won't be a moment."

Well, what did I care if he found my taste a bit flamboyant? He was being polite about it, anyway. I was glad he had remembered the coat; I was beginning to shiver as the cold of ancient stones encircled me.

This was the oldest part of the cathedral, the choir transept leading to the old cloister. The cloister itself, save for part of the old scriptorium and the boundary walls, had fallen to ruin centuries ago after the dissolution of the abbeys, leaving only a few moss-covered stumps of arches to bear witness to Henry VIII's devastation. The Norman transept, however, had survived intact, lone remnant of the eleventh-century church. Impressionable folk claimed they sometimes saw a monk here, robed and cowled, walking sadly and silently the steps he had trod so many hundred years before. I devoutly wished I hadn't remembered that story at just that moment.

The dark quiet was oppressive. Although hundreds of people still filled the huge nave, the cathedral's design funneled the sound away from this remote area, where the loudest noise was the echo of my own footsteps. I shivered again, not from cold this time, and then remembered the tiny flashlight in my bag. If only the batteries were still good . . . I rummaged, finally found it, and turned it on. Well, not exactly a spotlight, but at any rate a reassuring token of the twentieth century.

I took a firmer grip on it and inched toward the cloister door. If I opened it the outside light would brighten the area, and I didn't think I could get much colder. It wasn't easy to get my bearings in the looming dark. Surely the Fitzalan chantry was just here on the left, and then the last of the side chapels before the door? The frail beam of light confirmed my rapidly diminishing sense of direction. But then—there were no memorial brasses here, were there? That gleam of metal on the floor—what on earth?

It was a candlestick. My flashlight, with the perversity of its kind, brightened for a moment and then dimmed to a mere glimmer, but the brief flare was enough to show me the unmistakable silver shape. Ornate, three feet tall, it belonged with its mate on the altar of the lovely little chapel that should be here, just next to the cloister door. I picked up the heavy object, wondering why it was there, and moved forward to replace it.

"Mrs. Martin?"

I turned to Mr. Nesbitt's voice. "I'm over here, by the door. Can you see my flashlight?" Still moving as I looked back, I stumbled over something at the foot of the altar. Why, someone had left a bundle of vestments there! Or could it be. . . ? As I fought for balance the tiny flashlight flew from my hand, brightened again, and swung its light crazily over the scene. The last thing I saw before it fell and extinguished itself for good was yet another gleam. The gleam, from among the heap of garments, of a fixed and staring eye.

2

MY RECOLLECTION OF what came next is spotty, a series of images, snippets of sight and sound, each as hard-edged and vivid as a flash photograph.

The first memory is the scream, an obscene sound, a terrifying, shocking outrage that crashed off stone walls, echoed and re-echoed from vault to pavement, splintering the Christmas peace. Only when Mr. Nesbitt reached me and took both my arms in his strong hands did I realize it was I who was desecrating the night. The sudden knowledge that one is making an utter fool of oneself can be as effective against hysteria as a wet towel in the face. I stopped with a kind of strangled gargle, gulped once or twice, and tried to speak.

"I—is it—" My voice trembled as much as my knees. This was ridiculous. Pull yourself together, old girl. I took several deep breaths, hugged myself tightly, and tried again, without much more success. "I can't quite see—but there's—something—"

"Sit down." It was not a suggestion. He lowered me firmly to the floor. "Stay there." I suppose I obeyed, but this is one of the transitions I've lost. The next I remember, I was standing up and someone had organized some light—feeble but blessed—and people were gathering.

I saw the dean, half in and half out of his cassock, his clerical collar springing wildly free of a single button, but with dignity and authority unimpaired. The growing crowd—vergers, clergy, a few straggling parishioners, the choirmaster, and a gaggle of eager choirboys—parted like the Red Sea as he moved quietly through them, his raised hand stopping the boys in their tracks.

"Why, Mrs. Martin," he said mildly. "Whatever is the matter?"

Several hundred watts of electricity could hardly have dispelled the age-old shadows; a single lantern was woefully inadequate. But what light there was gave me, in one horrifying instant, an all-too-clear picture of the thing lying at the foot of the altar. I tried to speak, but the thin thread of sound couldn't be heard beyond my own lips.

It was Mr. Nesbitt who said, as one accustomed to being obeyed, "You'd better send the boys away, Dean." He had moved to block their view. "We have something of a problem here. Will you and one of the vergers stay, please, while I call for some assistance. No one must touch anything. And perhaps someone—oh, Margaret, good. Could you take Mrs. Martin to some place where she'll be comfortable, and stay with her for a bit? She's had a nasty shock."

Authority recognizes authority. Margaret Allenby, the dean's wife, moved toward me while the dean gave the choirboys into the keeping of their director and shooed the lot on their reluctant way. Then as he came closer his face turned so white that I started babbling. "It's all right, Dean. I mean it's not the ghost or anything. It's just a real person, a real dead person, that is. I think it must be Canon Billings, you see, and surely nobody could look like that and be alive, could they?" At the end of which remarkably silly speech I looked down again at the cassock on the floor, and the thing in it, and everything began to collapse in on itself and draw down to a single point of bright light.

I INSIST THAT I didn't quite faint. I'm *not* a fainting person. The idea made me so indignant that I rallied a bit. Someone, probably the dean's wife, shoved me down onto the altar rail and pushed my head between my knees, and the world opened out again. But it apparently took me a while to focus, because by the time I realized how extraordinarily uncomfortable I was and tried to get off that miserable stone perch, nearly everyone had gone. Mrs. Allenby was sitting awkwardly beside me, an arm around my shoulders to make sure I didn't fall, while the dean, with a green-faced junior verger, kept watch over the body. The dean looked extremely tired and worried, but his lips moved silently and I realized that he was performing part of his ritual for the dead.

"There, now," said Mrs. Allenby as I raised my head. "Feeling better, are you, dear?"

"I'm fine," I lied. I cleared my throat. "Fine. Really. I think I'd better stand up, though. My bones won't take that rail anymore." My firm assertion of independence was spoiled by a totter that nearly landed me on the floor. Mrs. Allenby tactfully held me up until I could stand more or less on my own two feet. This time I kept my eyes steadfastly away from the foot of the altar.

"Well, my dear, what a frightful thing!" Mrs. Allenby launched into a gentle flow of talk, insulating me with words from too much thought. "I'm sure I don't know *what* I'd have done, finding him like that, poor man. Now you're to come with me—can you walk a bit, do you think?—and have a little restorative. I know they *say* it isn't the thing, but I maintain a spot of brandy is steadying in a crisis, and Kenneth always keeps some here, because you never know, do you? That's right, just round

old Stephen's tomb, *here* we are. That's the most comfortable chair; I know it looks ready for the scrap heap, but
it's lovely to sit in, at least till it comes to the getting out,
and then I always need a hand up. Now you drink this
right down."

She handed me a small glass of liquid fire, and if I didn't
drink it right down, I certainly sipped gratefully, and it
helped.

As did my surroundings. I was in the small room set
aside for people who turned up at the cathedral with
problems too urgent to wait for an appointment with one
of the clergy in his own office. The room was a perfect
example of that kind of dignified, self-assured shabbiness
that the English upper classes specialize in. A faded,
once-fine rug lay on the floor. Cracked leather chairs provided, as promised, solid comfort. It was a pity the fireplace held only an electric heater instead of the crackling
logs that belonged there, but the warmth was welcome. It
seemed a place of peace and rather solemn good cheer.

After an interval the dean entered the room, his calm,
quiet manner not quite hiding his worry. Accustomed all
his life to dealing with human failings, familiar with
every sin in the calendar, he was nevertheless badly
shaken by the sudden death of his own canon in his own
cathedral. He came straight to me, with Mr. Nesbitt right
behind him.

"I see my wife is looking after you, Mrs. Martin." His
voice was filled with sad kindness. "I'm so sorry you
should have had this dreadful experience. Are you feeling
better?"

"Quite all right, thank you." Social lies are useful; if
you say often enough that things are fine you may begin
to believe it. "But, oh, Dean, I'm sorry I made such a fool
of myself. I suppose everyone in the place heard—"

"No, dear," said Mrs. Allenby soothingly. "The acoustics in this place are very odd. I shouldn't think anyone in

the nave heard a thing, and we managed to shoo away most of the people who turned up. And how could you possibly help it? I'm sure it would have been a terrible shock to anyone, finding him in the dark that way."

Mr. Nesbitt cleared his throat, and the dean took over.

"Yes, of course, Alan. I'm afraid, Mrs. Martin, if you're really feeling yourself again, there are some questions Mr. Nesbitt needs to ask you. This is the chief constable of Sherebury, who happened to be in church tonight, and came round to help. . . ."

"We've met," I said, pleased to hear that my voice sounded almost normal. "But why . . . ?"

"The police in this country," Mr. Nesbitt began, "as you may not know, Mrs. Martin, must investigate all cases of sudden death, even when we have no reason to believe it's anything but an accident." He sounded apologetic. "It's a shocking time of night, I know, and I do quite realize that you're feeling a trifle upset, but I'd like to ask you just one or two questions."

I was flooded with instant, foolish apprehension. How many mysteries had I read with just those words addressed to the chief suspect? Idiotic as it was, I had to swallow hard before I could respond with anxious cooperation.

"Of course I'll do anything I can to help. Not that I really know anything, but ask whatever you like."

"For a start, how did you happen to—be in the chapel? It's out of your way to the door."

I felt sure he had started to ask how I happened to fall over the body, and I was grateful for the euphemism. "Oh, that was the candlestick. It was on the floor, and it glimmered, sort of, in the light of my flashlight. So I picked it up to put it back . . ."

"Pity you picked it up, in the circumstances, but a perfectly natural thing to do. Can you show us, later, just where it was?"

That little shudder of apprehension came again. I tried to ignore it. "It was awfully dark, but I'll try. Oh, for heaven's sake, what did I *do* with it? It was heavy, I remember—I suppose I dropped it when—"

"It's all right, dear." Margaret Allenby intervened again. "You did drop it, but we found it, it's quite all right. It fell on—that is, it wasn't dented, or anything of that sort. I always thought that pair particularly hideous, anyway."

I didn't care to follow up all the non sequiturs in that speech, and apparently Mr. Nesbitt didn't either. He sighed. "If you can show me where you put it, Margaret, I'll have to have it checked for fingerprints. Not a bit of use, of course, that heavy carving won't show a thing, but one goes through the motions. I'm afraid I'll have to have your fingerprints as well, if you handled it, and Mrs. Martin's. For comparison."

My nerves tightened another notch, but Mr. Nesbitt let that drop for the moment and addressed the dean.

"Now, Kenneth, if I might just ask about the door to the cloisters. Isn't it usually kept unlocked?"

"Usually, but not lately," the dean answered promptly, as I registered the first-name basis, concentrating on the apparent social standing of chief constables to avoid more uncomfortable thoughts. "With the electrical work they're doing in that transept, it's so dark we didn't think it safe for the public at night. Of course all the doors, the public ones at any rate, have new locks so that they can always be opened from inside. In case of fire, you know. I must say I wasn't sorry to abandon the old keys, great medieval things a foot long that weighed pounds! We kept them, naturally; they're in a display case in the library. I'm so sorry, Alan," he added, catching Mr. Nesbitt's eye. "You're not interested in my keys."

"Well, not the old ones, actually, but I do need to know who has a key—a new key—to that door."

"Yes. I have a complete set, naturally. The rest of the clergy and staff have only the ones they need. To tell the truth I'm not really sure exactly who has what; there are so many people involved and the head verger looks after that side of things. I know Canon Billings often used the cloister door, since his house is on that side of the Close, so he probably had a key. Mr. Swansworthy will know."

I rather doubted that. The head verger was nearly eighty and definitely past most of his duties, but he stubbornly refused to retire and the dean was too softhearted to insist. It seemed to me most unlikely that he kept close track of the keys. However, it was none of my business, and I was far too tired to bring up anything that might keep me there any longer than necessary.

The dean went on. "I do see, of course, what you're getting at. This is certainly more your province than mine, but I should imagine the canon let himself in that door and then stumbled over something in the dark and hit his head. I blame myself very much for not organizing a small light—"

His wife interrupted. "Now, Kenneth, you know perfectly well it's not your fault. If Jonathan Billings had been where he was supposed to be, getting ready for the service . . ." Her tone left no doubt about her opinion of the unfortunate canon, and the dean sighed.

"But, my dear, we don't know when he came in. When we missed him, just before midnight Mass, nobody remembered seeing him for hours. And darkness comes early at this time of year. He might have been on his way *out*, after the children's service, for a cup of tea."

Mr. Nesbitt nodded. "In fact, I think he has been dead for some time. The medical examiner will be able to tell us more definitely, but I should say five or six hours at least. So you may be quite right, although if that's the case, I do rather wonder why he wasn't found earlier. Did you look for him yourself?"

"I had a quick look round, but of course I had to pre-pare for the service. I believe the vergers did rather a thorough search, at least so far as it's possible to search a place like this in a hurry and in the dark. No one knew what to think when he turned up missing; it was com-pletely unlike him to be irresponsible." So that's what the vergers had been up to when I was trying to find a seat. All except for the officious Mr. Wallingford, who found dripping candles more important than a missing canon.

"Well," said Mr. Nesbitt with the hint of a sigh, "we'll have to go a bit further into the search, as well as the mat-ter of when he was last seen alive, but I think morning will do for those things."

The dean looked startled. "Not *this* morning, surely. That is—Christmas Day?"

"We'll make it as brief as possible, I promise, and as discreet. I'm sure you realize we must collect as much data as possible while memories are still fresh. We'll save everything we can for Saturday and push on with other things, meanwhile." He hesitated for a moment. "I'm truly sorry, Kenneth. I know it seems unnecessarily intru-sive, but rules are rules; we do have to try to establish the cause of death. You can trust me to make sure my men don't make more of a nuisance of themselves than they have to."

He took a deep breath, turning back to me, and I saw how tired he looked. "Mrs. Martin, I know this may be difficult for you, but may I ask if you touched or moved the body at all?"

I had to swallow hard before I could deal with that one. "Well, I certainly touched it. I—I kicked it. That is, I stumbled over the cassock, in the dark. That's how I found it—him." I willed my hands to stop shaking while I sipped a little more brandy, spilling only a drop or two. "Thank God I didn't fall on top of him! I don't think I dis-turbed anything much, but I really can't tell you. It was pitch dark and then, later, I was—upset." There was a nice English understatement for them.

"I understand; try not to worry about it." He flexed his broad shoulders a little and ran a hand across the back of his neck. "I should think that's nearly all for now, then, if you can just show me where you found the candlestick."

I tried, unsuccessfully, not to remember the way Canon Billings had looked. "Is he still there? I mean—do I have to—"

"He's decently covered now, dear," said Mrs. Allenby. "She won't need to see him, will she, Alan?"

"Certainly not. Now, if you're feeling well enough?"

I rose, a bit unsteadily, I fear, brushing my skirt into place. "Yes. Well. Let's get it over with."

We trooped back down the dark, echoing corridor, past tombs and monuments that cast oddly shaped shadows, to the ancient transept.

In the brief time we had been away the area had been transformed. Bright, harsh lights stood on tall stands, their long cables snaking away to wherever they could connect with live electricity. Yellow plastic tape draped around portable stanchions turned the little jewel of a chapel into a "Crime Scene Do Not Enter," and a burly constable stood impassively enforcing the regulation—against no one, apparently; the transept was deserted, save for two other uniformed men.

"Crime scene?" I said uncertainly. "But surely . . ."

"It comes printed that way," said Mr. Nesbitt. "A trifle sensational, I agree, but the easiest, quickest way to isolate the area. Now if we could just . . ."

Canon Billings lay spotlighted where I had found him, but mercifully covered with a piece of cloth—a funeral pall, I saw as I moved closer. Appropriate.

"The candlestick was about here, I think, Mr. Nesbitt." I pointed to a spot on the floor about a foot from the body, just outside the doorway in the lacy screen that separated the chapel from the transept. "It really is hard to say. It was *very* dark, and I only had my flashlight. I wonder where my flashlight *is*, by the way. It must have rolled over there . . ." I peered into the shadows.

"We found the torch, Mrs. Martin. It's broken, I'm afraid. I shall be glad to have it repaired for you and return it. About here, you say?"

The constable marked it with chalk at my nod.

Mr. Nesbitt hadn't forgotten the fingerprints. One of the other uniformed men took me aside, and then Mrs. Allenby, and rolled our fingers on an inked pad and then on a card. He was extremely polite, offering a solvent-soaked rag to clean our fingers—which didn't make me feel a bit better.

The chief constable was apologetic when I came back to the little group.

"That's all I need, then, Mrs. Martin. I must apologize for keeping you here so long. I'm afraid this has all been very trying for you. I may need some more information a bit later, if there are any complications, but it seems straightforward enough." He surveyed the scene once more and then smiled wearily at us all. "Now I think we can all go home."

The dean's sense of duty kept him at the scene with the unhappy constable until the canon's body could be taken away, and Mrs. Allenby's loyalty kept her by his side. So only the chief constable and I, finally, stepped out through the cloister doorway into the night.

The rain had stopped, along with the wind, but a nip of frost sharpened the still air. I found myself grateful for the Burberry Mr. Nesbitt had retrieved and somehow held on to through all the confusion. The quiet was desolate; I shivered.

"You need your hat," he said, holding it out. "It fell off when—earlier."

I took it, jammed it on backward, and cleared my

throat. "I'm not sure it's the sort of hat a person could be said to 'need,' but thank you." The bit of frivolous nonsense had become woefully inappropriate.

We walked wordlessly past the ancient cemetery that dominated this part of the Close. The silence loomed. I was conscious of the squeak in one of my shoes.

I cleared my throat again. "Look, Mr. Nesbitt. I'm very grateful for your courtesy, but I don't need to be seen home. I can see my house from here. It's terribly late, actually Christmas day, and your family . . ."

"I live alone." His tone was almost curt. "My wife died some years ago and my children have left home."

"Oh, I see," I answered lamely. We plodded on in silence.

My house sits just beyond the wall of the Close, through a small gate. As we entered the little porch with its cushioned benches on each side, a big gray cat jumped down with loud, indignant cries. A fine time of night to be coming home, she scolded in mews as plain as English. Let a cat catch her death of cold in the rain. What's more, she hadn't been fed for a fortnight.

"I'm not impressed, Esmeralda," I said as I unlocked the door, grateful for the diversion. "It's what you get for not coming when I called you. Anyway I'll bet you've been asleep right here the whole time. And if you want to convince anyone you're starving, you're really going to have to lose some weight." I scooped her up, and she squeezed her huge green eyes shut, nestled against my chin, and purred in a comforting way.

Mr. Nesbitt smiled. "I see you have a most solicitous friend. You'll be all right, will you?"

"I'll be fine. I—Mr. Nesbitt, I didn't mean to be rude, or to pry into your personal affairs. You've been very kind, and I do thank you." I shifted Emmy and held out my hand.

"Not at all," he murmured, shaking my proffered

hand. "You—that is, I hope you have some plans for tomorrow? Today, that is? I shouldn't like to think—"

"Yes, indeed," I said quickly. "I have some friends coming for dinner. In—" I looked at my watch "—oh, goodness, in less than twelve hours!"

Once more it was the wrong thing to say. Here's your hat, what's your hurry. Mr. Nesbitt shook hands again.

"I must be getting home. I hope you can forget this unpleasantness quickly. Oh, here's your umbrella. Good night."

He turned away.

"I don't suppose you'd like to come to Christmas dinner?" It came out before I knew I was going to say it. "I mean, if you don't have other plans? I always cook way too much food."

His smile was warmly genuine; the chief constable submerged once more beneath the human being. "Thank you so much. I'll be spending the day with my married daughter, but it's kind of you to think of me. Get some sleep, won't you?" And he walked back into the Close, his footsteps ringing on the paving stones.

I stood at the door watching him until Emmy reminded me that it was late, and she was cold, hungry, and tired of being held. When at last I shut the door, she wriggled out of my arms and gave me one quizzical look before marching purposefully to the kitchen.

I gave her a little leftover ham just to keep the peace, and dropped into a kitchen chair. I ought to go to bed, I thought. I ought to do a dozen small chores before I go to bed. I sat.

At least it was almost warm. Through the centuries of additions and alterations to my rented Jacobean house, no one has seen fit to put in central heating. They simply added on electrical gadgets whose cost threatens to send me back to America. So the only place in the house I can afford to heat is the kitchen, where a large coal-burning

Aga stove holds sway in the huge old fireplace. It has me thoroughly cowed. I don't always stoke it properly, and I'm far too timid to cook anything complicated on it, so I've established a borrowed electric stove in a corner. But as long as the Aga's purring away, there's a tank full of hot water for tea, a place to dry the dish towels, and a gentle warmth in my kitchen.

My head nodded forward, and I caught myself with a jerk. Those chores could wait. Emmy thought so too. She led the way as I dragged myself up the steep, narrow steps to bed, and then settled in purring at my feet the moment I pulled up the covers. I thought I was too tired to sleep at all. In fact I dropped at once fathoms deep into a place where dead men walked in monks' cowls and lay on the cold stones with cats licking their faces.

༄3༄

ONE OF THE cats became more and more insistent and turned into Esmeralda, lying on my chest purring loudly and cleaning my chin with her sandpaper tongue. When I tried to push her away she became even heavier and entirely immovable.

I opened my eyes with the greatest reluctance. It was still quite dark, but morning comes late to northern countries in December. I knew Emmy was right. Her breakfast was long overdue, and other duties awaited me as well. It was Christmas.

I groaned and turned over, spilling the cat from my chest as I buried my face in the pillow. I had been dreading this day. Holidays are the hardest times, and Christmas, with its load of happy associations, seemed likely to be the worst of all. Knowing I didn't dare let myself think too much, I had deliberately planned a busy day. Preparing an elaborate meal in an unfamiliar kitchen ought to be enough of a challenge to occupy my mind, I had thought.

I hadn't counted on a horrible experience the night before, nor on a drastically shortened night's sleep. I wanted desperately to go back to sleep with the covers over my head and wake up when Christmas was over.

Emmy, more practical, jumped on the bed again with

enough force to set the springs creaking, and swatted my hair energetically. There was no help for it. I pushed myself up and found my glasses.

"Mrraow!" Emmy urged, heading for the door.

"Yes, well, Merry Christmas to you, too," I said sourly, and reached for my robe and slippers.

The bedroom was freezing. It must have turned much colder in the night. In no mood to consider economy, I turned on every electric heater I passed on my way downstairs and hoped I wouldn't blow a fuse or burn the house down.

Thank God for the Aga, anyway, and its warmth and hot water for the kettle. By the time I'd fed the frantic cat, the water was boiling, and with tea and toast inside me I began to feel almost human. A nice hot bath would complete the process, and surely the water heater I'd switched on upstairs must have done its job by now.

It had, and the bath was certainly warming, but it was a mistake all the same. Leisurely baths allow far too much thinking time. As hard as I tried to turn my thoughts to pleasant channels, they kept slipping from my grasp and returning to the two subjects I most wanted to forget. Last Christmas. And last night. A tear slipped down my cheek, and another, and several more. . . .

The phone rang.

I gripped my towel and sprinted, and tried to clear the tears out of my voice. "Hello?"

"Good morning, my dear. I hope I didn't ring up at an awkward time, or get you out of bed?"

"Dr. Temple! How lovely to hear from you! No, I was just getting out of the tub." Well, I should have been, anyway. I blotted with one hand, ineffectually.

"Ah. I shan't keep you, then. I just rang you up to wish you a very Merry Christmas indeed, and ask you to come round when you can, tomorrow or next week; I've a tiny gift for you."

"That's—very kind of you." I was still having a little trouble with my voice. "I'll do that. And Merry Christmas to you, too."

Well! That was unexpectedly pleasant. Dr. Temple was a darling, one of the people who had made our first long stay in Sherebury so agreeable. Frank had been on sabbatical from Randolph, the Midwestern university where he taught biology, and we'd come to England for his research. It happened that the University of Sherebury had just the resources he needed. Although one of the so-called 'red-brick universities'—as opposed to 'Oxbridge'—it was a well-respected institution, its architecture a mixture of pleasant Victorian extravagance and blocky modern practicality, with very few red bricks in evidence. Dr. Temple, the head of an excellent biology department, had shown Frank the ropes and introduced us to everyone in town. In his eighties now and slowing down a bit, he still kept an avuncular eye on me. He was the only one from the university, really, who still treated me like a person now that Frank was gone.

He was, in fact, a real friend. That made two, with Jane. Beyond that—no, it was foolish to think about friends just now. Or the lack of them. The phone call had cheered me up, and I'd better just accept the blessing and get on with what I had to do.

Which was suddenly far too much; I was way behind schedule. Dinner was set for two o'clock, and even for only three guests—Jane and two American friends who live in London—I was cooking enough for an army. Habit. At home there had always been lots of people— friends, relatives, students. . . .

Stop that, now, I scolded myself, and go stuff the blasted turkey.

When I was done in the kitchen I had to hang the wreath on the door and put a few more ornaments on the tree, the cherished old baubles Frank and I had collected . . . don't think about that, either; stay cheerful.

I'm not sure when the bells began to ring. Living so close to the cathedral I had become accustomed to them, although they used to startle me enormously. But today they overpowered the clamor of my thoughts. They were ringing the Christmas peal, and that took my mind back to last night's bells. It had been a beautiful service, really. I remembered, dreamily, the look of the vast church lit only by candles, and the sound of the choir and that magnificent organ, and the silly pomposity of the bishop on his throne. . . .

I giggled aloud and Emmy, who had been watching my mood, took the laugh as an invitation to play. I was trying by that time to lay a fire, a proper wood fire, in what I prefer to call my parlor. Emmy loved the idea of the fire, or rather she liked the lovely rustle of the newspaper as I crinkled it up. She kept leaping into the grate to capture what she was convinced were cat toys and streak off with them. "Emmy, you fiend! Bring that back here!" I tore after her as she leaped onto the hall rug, prize firmly clenched between her teeth, and stopped dead, four legs stiffly extended. The rug, however, kept going on the polished boards, and Emmy, rug, and newspaper careered into the umbrella stand, which fell over with a clatter that sent Emmy up the stairs. I cleared up the mess, still laughing, and blessed the day that a furry comedian had come into my life.

Glancing out the window I wished once more that it would *snow* instead of just glooming all day. Snow would be so pretty on the ancient slate roof of my little house, would contrast so beautifully with the tiny pink handmade bricks. Snow was *right* for Christmas, but it looked as if we weren't going to get any.

By the time I got myself into party clothes, the plum pudding reheating in the steamer was adding its sweet clove-and-cinnamon aroma to the fragrance of sage and onion and the heady pine scent of the tree. I lit the fire,

the doorbell signaled the arrival of my company, and it
was—indisputably, wonderfully—Christmas.

"Hey, how's my best girl?" boomed Tom Anderson,
enveloping me in a bear hug smelling of expensive after-
shave the moment I got the door open. "Wow, look at
you, gorgeous!" He held me out at arm's length, surveyed
my lacy Victorian blouse and long red velvet skirt, and
awarded a wolf whistle.

"Dorothy, I'm *consumed* with envy!" said his wife,
Lynn, a slim brunette with a high polish and a Katharine
Hepburn accent and nothing to fear from any woman.
She wasn't, of course, looking at me and Tom. "*What* a
marvelous house!"

Lynn and Tom live in the Belgravia section of London
in a house straight out of *Upstairs, Downstairs*. I dropped a
curtsy. "Thank you for them kind words, m'lady. I'm glad
you two finally got here to see it before the electric bills
drive me out. Do you want a drink first, or the grand
tour?"

"Drink," said Tom, at the same instant Lynn said "Tour."

"Okay," said Tom amiably. "I'll do the drinks while
you kids worship the architecture. Point me in the right
direction, D. You want the usual?"

"In the kitchen, the cabinet over the fridge. Through
there. I'll have whatever's in that suspicious-looking parcel under your arm." I knew perfectly well it was a bottle
of Jack Daniel's, which Tom picks up for me at duty-free
prices when he goes back to the States on business.
Wealth hasn't spoiled Tom's eye for a bargain, and he
shares my weakness for the sour-mash bourbon that's
scarce and expensive in England.

"C'mon, Dorothy, the *house*!"

"Monkswell Lodge," I began in my best National Trust
manner, "was built in 1607 to serve as the gatehouse for
Lord William Fitzhenry, who had lived in the monastery
buildings since the Dissolution. It is named after

Monkswell Street, which in turn comes from the fact that
the well serving the abbey was situated—"

"Come off it, and tell me about these *delectable*
leaded-glass windows. How do you ever keep them
clean?"

"I don't, as you would see if the sun were shining. But
the real gem of the house, outside the wonderful old
kitchen, is the bedroom ceiling. . . ."

"I ADORE THE name, Monkswell Lodge!" said Lynn
with an artistic shiver when we were back in the parlor.
Reminds me of Monkswell Manor in *The Mousetrap*."

Lynn loves the classic English mystery as much as I do;
we met at a convention of the Dorothy L. Sayers Society,
but her real favorite is Agatha Christie. "Now can't you
just see this place, isolated by the snow—"

"Humph!" I interrupted. "*What* snow, I'd like to know!"

"Speaking of snow," said Tom meaningfully.

"Oh!" Lynn dived into her carryall, coming up with a
box. "Merry Christmas and all that. I almost forgot."

I've always been a kid about presents. I tore into the
wrapping. A box, a smaller box, lots of shredded tissue—
ah. I lifted it out, balancing it in my palms.

It was a snowstorm, a big one with a Victorian look.
The heavy carved base supported a glass globe in which
two china children were building a snowman. When I
shook it gently the snow whirled in a most satisfactory
blizzard and then settled, leaving little white pyramids on
the snowman and the children's hats.

"Now where did you find something so perfect?"

"Oh, it's from my family, actually. I got it the last time
we went home, but it didn't really go with my house, and
we thought you'd love it."

"I do." I shook it again. No, it wouldn't fit in very well
with the Andersons' Sargents and Renoirs, which, given

Tom's exalted position with one of the multinational con-
glomerates, were very likely real. But it would be perfect
with the homely objects on my mantel. I set it in place
carefully and hugged Lynn with real gratitude for both
gift and friendship.

I had just handed over the stollen I'd baked for them
when Jane arrived with her contribution, a big box of
Christmas crackers.

I've loved crackers ever since my first English
Christmas years ago, when I learned the word didn't refer
to anything edible, but to party favors. The sharp crack
when you pull them, the smell of fireworks, the silly hats
and toys inside and even the terrible jokes, all seem very
festive and English. As soon as introductions were over
and I'd given Jane a drink, we got down to serious fun.
We went through the whole dozen, solemnly reading out
things like, "What's Christmas when the pump runs dry?
No-well!" to a chorus of groans.

"I'm absolutely going to have to get some of these for
next year," I said finally, putting my minute plastic
Christmas tree under the big one and settling my paper
crown more firmly on my head.

"Come to the Christmas sales on Monday and get
some at Harrod's," suggested Lynn. "They'll be on sale,
and they're the best—little silver toys in them. And we'll
treat you to tea at the Ritz. How about it?"

"I can't afford the best ones even at sale prices, but
that's a really good idea all the same. I might find a bargain in an electric blanket; that nice picturesque bedroom
of mine is becoming arctic. And tea at the Ritz is my idea
of the ultimate sinful luxury. Done."

We all wore our crowns in to dinner, which was, if I do
say so myself, superb—a traditional Christmas dinner
with a distinctly American accent until we came to
dessert. I brought in the plum pudding properly aflame,
to the proper applause.

"Jane, Lynn, you're going to have to take some of this home with you," I said when we had eaten ourselves to a complete stop. "I can*not* eat up three-fourths of a plum pudding by myself."

"Good," said Jane promptly. "Some of the kids are coming in for tea next week; I'll feed it to them. They're always starving at that age."

"Speaking of kids," I said lazily, "there was one with you last night at church who looked as if he might really *be* starving. I've never seen him before—dark, intense, good-looking—a striking boy. Is he one of your 'old boys'?"

"Nigel Evans. No, he came to town just a few months ago. To the university. Don't know him well, myself. Sat next to him last night to try to talk, but he's quiet. Supposed to be brilliant, but rebellious. He'll get over it, they always do, the clever ones. Poor as a church mouse, I hear, and makes it worse by spending every cent on Inga Endicott over at the Rose and Crown."

"She's a very pretty girl," I said tolerantly.

"Sensible girl," said Jane, from whom it was the highest compliment. "Won't have much to do with that lad until he settles down, I shouldn't have thought."

"And meanwhile he's squandering his substance on her?"

"What substance he has: not a lot. An orphan, lives from hand to mouth. Thought you'd have seen him at the cathedral. Works in the library."

"I've never spent much time in the library. I don't care for Canon Billings. Didn't, I should say." A little shudder ran up my spine, but I was too full of dinner and Christmas comfort to get a full attack of the horrors.

Lynn looked at me curiously. "Has your canon retired, then?"

"Not exactly retired," said Jane dryly. "Dead. Some sort of accident in the cathedral. Dorothy knows more about it than I do."

I didn't question what Jane knew, or how. Jane knows everything that goes on in Sherebury, by osmosis, I think.

"I don't know anything, really," I protested. "I just had the bad luck to find the body. After church, last night."

"But how awful!" said Lynn. "What on earth happened?"

"If you don't want to talk about it . . ." Tom spoke quietly, his eyes fixed on me, and Lynn looked abashed.

"No, I don't mind, really," I said, and found to my surprise that it was almost true. "I just honestly don't know what happened. He was on the floor, with a candlestick beside him, and his head was . . ." I trailed off and started again. "I imagine he either fell and hit his head on the floor, or somehow managed to hit himself with the candlestick. They're heavy and badly balanced. I know, because I picked it up."

"It doesn't sound very likely," said Lynn thoughtfully. "I mean, how do you hit yourself on the head with something by accident? Maybe somebody did him in!" Her eyes were beginning to sparkle. *"Murder in the Cathedral!* No, that was Becket, wasn't it?"

"I don't think Canon Billings was any saint," I said, smiling. "He wasn't very popular, the little I know about it. But I seriously doubt anyone hated him enough to bash him on the head with a candlestick."

"Speaking of candlesticks," said Tom, "do you still play Clue?"

"Now you're talking!" I rummaged about and found the set, and the four of us pursued Colonel Mustard, Mrs. Peacock, et al., through the rooms of poor Mr. Boddy's mansion for a couple of delightful hours.

It was after six and the early-December evening was upon us when my guests finally left. I was tired but content. It had been a lovely Christmas, after all. It was nearly time for supper, really, but I couldn't eat a thing and there were small chores to be done. I tidied the parlor a bit, threw scraps of wrapping paper and bits of exploded crackers in the fire Tom had rebuilt for me before they left, and collapsed in the most comfortable chair with a thimbleful of brandy. Emmy jumped into my lap and immediately went to sleep, full of turkey. I thought idly about getting an Agatha Christie or a Dorothy Sayers to while away the evening, but I would have to wait until Emmy decided to move. Everyone knows it's terrible manners to disturb a sleeping cat. She'd leave soon. Meanwhile it was very relaxing just to pet her soft, warm fur and look into the fire. . . .

When I woke with a crick in my neck Emmy was long gone. The room was freezing; so was I. The fire had been dead for some time.

It was nearly ten. I was wide awake and hungry, so I turned on the TV for the evening news and went to fix myself (and Emmy, of course) some leftovers.

I'd missed the headline stories by the time I got back to the parlor, but I settled down with my plate to pay attention to what was left and catch the weather.

". . . quiet day in London, to the relief of police, who had prepared for terrorist attacks.

"In other news, foul play is suspected in the death of a Sherebury clergyman. The Reverend Canon Jonathan Billings, fifty-two, was found last night in Sherebury Cathedral dead of an injury to the head, and certain inconsistencies have launched a police inquiry. No one has as yet been detained for questioning.

"The weather for Boxing Day: cold and clear over much of southern England, with a deep depression and snow likely north of. . ."

I didn't hear the weather after all. I stared at Emmy, who stared unblinkingly back. Murder. I'd laughed at the idea with Lynn, so why did I have the feeling I'd known it all along?

⋘4⋙

BOXING DAY, December 26, dawned clear and cold, as promised. For anyone not yearning for snow, it was a glorious day. Esmeralda could hardly wait to be let out. The sunshine had brought noisy, squabbling birds to my feeder, and Emmy was itching to get at them. Fortunately she's much too fat and slow to be a threat to anything but the occasional naive mouse. I let her out and turned to my own chores for the day.

The house seemed awfully quiet as I moved about restlessly, flicking a dust cloth here and there. Emmy makes herself so much a presence in the house that without her my thoughts echoed.

And they were thoughts I didn't want to hear even once. At home, the day after Christmas, Frank and I would have been admiring our Christmas presents again, or laughing over the absurd ones. It was always a lazy day, no point in housecleaning with Christmas spread all over the place, no need to cook with all the leftovers in the house. We'd make turkey sandwiches and eat them sitting around the fireplace, rereading Christmas cards from old friends. . . .

I turned the radio up loud and tried to find something to do, but there didn't seem to be anything that mattered much. Aimlessly, I wandered into the small room I use as a library and stared at the shelves.

Everybody's written a Christmas mystery. Agatha Christie's *Holiday for Murder*. Ngaio Marsh's *Tied Up in Tinsel*. Ellis Peters's *Virgin in the Ice* and *Raven in the Foregate*. Dorothy L. Sayers's *The Nine Tailors*. I picked up *Rest You Merry* by that mistress of the ridiculous, Charlotte MacLeod, and chuckled again over the first few pages, where a respectable professor goes berserk over his Christmas decorations and drives the neighborhood crazy. Slipping into the squashy old armchair, I read on.

I had quite forgotten, until the words accosted me from the page, the cold, fishy stare the murder victim gives the professor as she lies dead on his living room floor. With something between a sigh and a gulp I closed the book. My mind's eye saw not Professor Shandy's living room, but a small chapel in Sherebury Cathedral, an eye gleaming out of the darkness, a crushed skull. . . .

It was from that precise moment, I realized much later, that my rehabilitation began. Something in my mind rebelled and I was, abruptly, furious with myself. When was I going to *stop* this self-pity and develop some backbone? Frank, bless his heart, was gone. And I'd had a terrible experience, literally stumbling over a body. Very well. I could continue to wallow in misery and use it as an excuse to avoid life. Or I could do something positive about my circumstances. A vague optimism stirring within me, I slammed the book shut and heaved myself out of my chair.

"I'll go see Dr. Temple, that's what I'll do! It's Boxing Day, after all." On the traditional English day for the exchanging of small Christmas courtesies I'd need, though, to take at least a token gift. There were those Christmas cookies I'd baked just to have on hand. I hastily wrapped a dozen of them, pulled on my warmest coat and a bright orange mohair hat, and set out.

It really *was* a gorgeous day. The town looked like a movie set. Most of the houses on my street are Georgian, built in one of Sherebury's most prosperous periods. At any time their red brick and white trim made them look fresh and tidy, but in the sunshine of that December day they might have been newly made from children's Christmas building sets. The crystal-cold light glinted and sparkled off brightly painted front doors, polished brass knobs, spanking clean bow windows. I found myself humming as I hurried along to Dr. Temple's, three streets away.

"My dear, what a delightful surprise! Come in, come in!" The old professor opened his door wide, letting me and a lot of cold air in and at the same time letting out his pair of indignant Siamese cats, who hated company.

"Will Soo and Ling be all right in all this cold?"

"They'll be back in a bit to sit staring at you cross-eyed, trying to make you go away. You remember their routine. Intimidating animals. Useful for unwanted guests, but a trifle embarrassing with friends. Now—coffee? I was just about to have some myself."

I followed Dr. Temple to his spotless kitchen. His little house, only a few years old, was as tidy as his scientific mind. Not for him the slipshod splendors of the past. "Have you the slightest idea," he had said when I moved into my ancient pile, "how many varieties of vermin can be found in your average picturesque dwelling? Give me a place I can keep clean." Many were the maiden ladies of Sherebury who had longed to capture this pearl, but the wily Dr. Temple had managed, with the help of Soo and Ling, to maintain both his bachelor independence and his reputation for cordiality, no mean feat.

I laid the package of cookies on the gleaming counter. "These might be good with the coffee."

"Splendid! Although I shall no doubt eat far more than I should. Alas!" He patted his stomach complacently, blue eyes twinkling at me over his granny glasses, white hair flying out of control as it always did when he was pleased.

"Nonsense. If you lost weight you wouldn't be half so effective playing Santa Claus."

"Well, my dear, the hair and the beard would still fit the part, and one could always wear padding. No, the real danger is that one day I shall actually outgrow the red suit, and then what's to be done, eh?"

We settled down with coffee and cookies at the kitchen table, where a tie box-shaped parcel lay wrapped in white tissue paper. "For you, my dear."

The box weighed virtually nothing and made no noise when I shook it. I looked up to see the twinkle much in evidence, but Dr. Temple refused to say a word, so I ripped off the paper, lifted the lid, and saw—

"Feathers?"

"Feathers. I find them, you know, when I go out birding. The pheasant you'll recognize, and the peacock—only a portion, that, I'm afraid. Poor fellow must have broken it off in a fight. And any number of small birds, common, but colorful."

I was still bewildered, and he chuckled.

"My dear, for your hats!"

"Of course! How stupid of me. They're the very thing; thank you so much!" I tucked the long pheasant feather into the brim of my orange hat, giving it a rakish look that pleased me very much.

"So. What's going on at the university these days?" Dr. Temple kept up with the gossip, though he'd held emeritus status for years.

"Well, we've lost a good teacher. But you'd know all about that."

"I would?"

"Canon Billings, my dear. You did know he taught a philosophy seminar, didn't you?"

"I had no idea. I didn't know the man at all, except to speak to. Was he really a good teacher? I wouldn't have thought . . ."

"In the sense that he was a first-rate scholar and lecturer, yes, he was. Not popular, of course, too sarcastic and superior for the students to like him, but they respected him."

"What about the rest of the staff? What did they think of him?"

"Not trying to do a little prying, are you, my dear? See yourself as an amateur sleuth?" The blue eyes were keen.

"Of course not," I said. Too quickly? "I'm curious, that's all. I do have a personal interest, after all."

"Of course." But the eyes stayed alert. "Actually most of the staff saw very little of him. The seminar was held evenings, naturally, since the canon had his duties during the day. I know old Pebmarsh thought a great deal of his abilities."

Dr. Pebmarsh, head of the philosophy department, was at least fifteen years Dr. Temple's junior. The use of "old," then, told me something, as did the rest of the cautious wording. As much as he loved gossip, the dear old professor hated to say anything bad about anyone. The fact that he hadn't been able to say anything really good . . .

"Have you seen George Chambers lately?" he asked, changing the subject.

"Christmas Eve, just for a moment, but not really to talk to. How's he getting along?"

"Not so very well, as I understand it. His lectures aren't well attended, I'm told. Of course George always was a bit pompous, and students don't like pomposity—excepting their own."

I laughed at that, and we discussed student politics over the last of the cookies. When imperious yowls indicated that the Siamese wanted in, I took the opportunity to slip away before Dr. Temple could work up to offering me lunch. I needed a good long walk to deal with all that butter and sugar.

The sun was still shining brightly, but there was a softer feeling to the air and a slight haze that told me rain might be on the way. Better enjoy Sherebury while the sun shone.

When Frank and I first visited England we got a little claustrophobic about all those houses with touching walls, opening directly onto the sidewalk. The place looked so different from the shady streets of Hillsburg, Indiana, our hometown. We longed for soft green front lawns with untidy rambler roses climbing over the railings of front porches hospitably furnished with swings and rockers. And maple trees that dropped bushels full of leaves to clean up in the fall, all the neighbors out at the same time, helping each other, and the lovely smell of burning leaves. And elms growing into graceful Gothic arches over the street. . . .

But Hillsburg's elm trees are all gone now, fallen to disease. Leaf burning is against the law, and neighborliness is disappearing, too, a victim of hurry and stress and fear. The big lawns that seemed so friendly when we were young serve to isolate people now; they've built high fences, and no one sits on the front porches. Small-town America isn't what it used to be.

Probably small-town England isn't either, but I didn't know it way back when, and there's a lot to be said for the way it is now. As I walked I watched the passing parade of humanity with appreciation. People greeted each other, smiling, asking about the health of mothers and spouses and offspring as if they really wanted to know. There seemed, in England, still to be a network of neighbors caring about each other. If only I could belong to that network . . . but even if I never did, quite, I was glad it existed. Maybe there was nothing momentous about being told what a beautiful day it was or asked how one was feeling, but small courtesies grease the machinery of life. In their own way, they're important.

Deep in thought, I rounded a corner and ran full tilt into a fellow pedestrian.

"Oh, I'm so sorry, it was my fault—oh, it's you, George. Dear me, did I do any damage?"

"No, no. Actually, I'm glad I—er—ran into you, Dorothy. I wanted to ask—" he looked around and lowered his voice "—how you're getting on. Unpleasant experience, discovering a body."

So George knew all about my involvement. So had Dr. Temple. I suppose by now everyone in town knew. No space-age communications network can compete with the one English cathedral towns have relied on from time immemorial.

Was there an answer to George's remarkable understatement? It didn't matter; he wasn't listening anyway.

"We thought—Alice and I—you might like to come to tea. If you've nothing planned, that is. Get away from it all for a bit, don't you know. Alice makes jolly good Christmas cake," he added enticingly.

I had to swallow a grin. Tea! The panacea for everything from weariness to a cold to murder. Some things about England never change, which is why I love it so much.

I considered. Poor old George *was* a bit of a bore, but he and his wife were kind to us in the old days. George, even though he was history and Frank was biology, had made a point of welcoming Frank at the university. And it was true that Alice made the best Christmas cake I'd ever tasted. Besides, if they were beginning to recognize my continued existence, for the first time, really, since Frank—well, I'd be stupid and ungrateful to turn down the invitation.

"Thank you, George, that's very kind of you. I'd love to come to tea. Five o'clock or so? I'll see you then."

• • •

I WAS GETTING fairly good at reading English weather. By the time I was ready to set out for tea the softness had turned, not yet to rain, but to an insidious fog that wrapped its clammy fingers around the town. Emmy had come in with several remarks about the damp and plumped herself down where she could dry her fur in front of the "electric fire," as the ugly little heater is euphemistically called. As I wrapped myself in various layers against the elements she looked up and uttered a brief but pungent comment.

"You're quite right. I'm an idiot, but I've said I'll go, so I have to. I promise I'll be back as soon as I can decently get away. You leave the tree alone, now." I gave one last longing look at the heater and let myself out into the raw dampness.

Familiar streets had turned strangely forbidding as the fog closed in, and I stumbled, trying to hurry, on obstacles that seemed to pop out of the pavement as I approached. It was a fair piece of a walk. George and Alice lived on the edge of town, close to the university, which is really outside Sherebury proper. Their house, a new one built at the end of an old street, is in the style that used to be called "stockbroker Tudor." To me it has always looked as out of place in its setting as a chorus girl among duchesses. It is undoubtedly bigger, more convenient, and easier to maintain than my own, which makes it even more unforgivable.

And you should be ashamed, Dorothy, I scolded myself. Here are nice people who've invited you over for the proverbial tea and sympathy, and you're criticizing their taste. All the same, as I knocked at their door I couldn't help smiling. The large, well-polished brass knocker in the shape of a lion with a ring in its mouth was so deliciously inappropriate for George's house.

Alice greeted me with such resolute charm and grace that I instantly wondered if the invitation had been her idea. Surely it would never have occurred to George that I might need some comfort.

Ensconced in an overstuffed chair while Alice went to cope with tea, I studied the room, redecorated since I had seen it last. I remembered the rumors that Alice had money. Somebody certainly had; George's job couldn't support them in this style. It looked straight out of *Architectural Digest* and made me profoundly uneasy, especially the white furniture, though blissfully comfortable. In this house stray cat hairs would not be looked upon with favor, and my dark slacks were, as usual, covered with gray fuzz.

Before I could tear apart the rest of the room, Alice and the cake entered to a silent fanfare of trumpets, followed by George with a heavily laden tea tray. His rather pink nose seemed to twitch slightly, and suddenly his graying fair hair, neat military mustache, and little academic potbelly reminded me irresistibly of the White Rabbit.

"Now that's what I like to see, a nice smile! Sorry to keep you waiting, my dear. Delighted you could come. But would you rather have a drop of something, eh? Mulled wine, whiskey?"

"No, no, tea is just right on a day like this, thank you." That sounded as if George *was* in charge of this meeting. Curiouser and curiouser. I furtively pulled an extra-large gray clump from the chair cushion and settled myself with my cup of tea and a sandwich or two.

"Now then, my dear, cheers, and the very best wishes of the season!" He lifted his teacup in salute. "And what on earth is all this nonsense about murder, eh?"

So that was it. Not compassion, curiosity. He wanted to hear all the gory details. Well, he was going to be disappointed. My resolve to be practical and positive about this murder didn't mean I had to wallow in gore for George's entertainment.

Alice was obviously horrified at George's idea of teatime conversation. She gave him a kick on the ankle that I wasn't supposed to see and changed the subject.

"I do hope you had a lovely Christmas, Dorothy. We're not doing you very well in the way of weather, are we? This foggy frost is so frightfully depressing, I always think."

Not very original, but I was happy to go along. "Oh, it is. Just like *A Christmas Carol*, at the beginning, you know, the part about 'foggier still, and colder.' I feel definitely cheated about snow. But yes, Christmas was very agreeable, thank you. I had people over for dinner, the Andersons, you remember them, don't you? And Jane Langland." I was prepared to regale them with a full description of the dinner menu, or anything else so long as it didn't have to do with bodies, but George was not to be diverted.

"Ah, yes, how did dear old Jane take it? The murder, I mean."

"Really, George!" But Alice sighed and picked up her teacup, recognizing defeat. When George climbs on a subject, I remembered from the old days, he rides it to death, and the quickest way to get it over with is to go along for the ride.

He was waiting for an answer. "I haven't the slightest idea," I responded shortly. "I haven't see her since I heard that it *was* murder. She didn't seem particularly devastated by his death, if that's what you mean. But why on earth should Jane 'take it' in any particular way? I didn't get the impression she was a particular friend of the canon."

"No, no, but I should have thought—that is, what with all those students hanging about—at least—"

"What *are* you talking about, George?" asked Alice,

very crisply indeed. One well-shod toe beat a tattoo against the carpet.

The White Rabbit's nose twitched again, and he cleared his throat self-importantly. "Jane's protégés, that's what. Surely it's occurred to you that Nigel Evans is one of the prime suspects, if Billings really was murdered?"

He sat back and sipped his tea, watching smugly for our reactions. Mine must have disappointed him: blank incomprehension.

"George, Nigel is only a name to me, and I don't have a clue as to what you mean. And he isn't one of Jane's 'protégés,' as you put it. I did ask her about him yesterday—no, not as a murder suspect, don't be silly," as his ears perked up. "I was interested because I saw him at the cathedral and he has such a striking face. She told me a little about him, but said she didn't know him very well. What on earth makes you think he could have—done something like that?" The words "kill" and "murder" were too embarrassing; they sounded like cheap melodrama, especially in Alice's highly refined room.

"Oh, I don't say he did. But he had reason. I suppose Jane told you, at least, that he worked for Billings?"

I nodded. "In the cathedral library."

"And did she tell you they had a blazing row the very day the good canon—died?"

Alice and I fastened our eyes on George with an attention that seemed to please him. He cleared his throat again.

"I presume you do know Evans is a student." He was going to make us wait for it.

"Jane told me he's at the university. She didn't say what he's studying."

"Reading history. Thinks he's God's gift to scholarship. Entirely above himself, that lad. If you ask me, he needs a good kick in the pants, which is just what he would have got if Billings hadn't died just now. He was about to be sent down."

"Sent down! Expelled, you mean? But surely not! Jane called him 'brilliant.'"

"That's as may be." George was getting worked up; his face was an alarming shade of purple. "He's bright enough, when he wants to be. He's also belligerent, rude, and too cocky by half."

"He's one of your students." It wasn't a question.

"Not mine, really. Worked with me from time to time, that's all, helped proofread my book for a little spare cash. Oh, I won't deny he's been a good student. Keen. But he'd got to the point where he knew a little about this and that, and thought he knew it all. Actually argued with me over some points in my book. He's twenty years old! I was reading history before he was born or thought of."

"Oh, for heaven's sake, George, rudeness is annoying, certainly, but the young *are* sure of themselves." And, I didn't say aloud, being rude to you is almost irresistible. "I can't believe that's enough to get him thrown out of school! He's not the first young man in a university to be rude."

"Of course that's not all of it," said George irritably. "I told you he had a row with Billings. Flinging accusations all over the shop, and the *language*! There would have been no choice but to report his shameful behavior to the university authorities, and what would they have done about it, I ask you?"

I was beginning not to like the smell of this. "What was the quarrel about, George?"

"Don't know," he admitted with some reluctance. "I was in the library at the time, in the stacks. Apparently they didn't see me. I couldn't actually hear what they said until they started shouting, and by that time it was all name-calling, or worse, and I wanted no part of it. But before I left I heard Evans threaten him. 'You'll regret it if you do, I promise you that.'"

"If everyone who made threats carried them out, the

undertakers couldn't keep up," I retorted. "Personally, I don't think the canon was murdered at all. It had to have been some sort of accident."

"Ah, yes, I wondered what you thought of it all," said George. "You know more than any of us, of course."

"I don't know a thing, except what I saw, and I don't want to talk about that." I felt I had made sufficient payment for my tea. "I don't even want to think about it. I simply can't believe anyone would kill a clergyman in his own church."

"It has been done," murmured Alice. "And Canon Billings was a much less popular man than Thomas à Becket. But Dorothy, you haven't had any Christmas cake. Do let me cut you some."

George opened his mouth but was quelled by a look that would have frozen warm Jell-O. Alice had had more than enough, and this time she intended to exercise her authority.

I was delighted to drop the subject and settle down to some cake, myself. English tea pastries are always wonderful, but at Christmastime they surpass themselves. You get miniature mince pies, extremely flaky and rich, and Christmas cake, which has no American equivalent. Alice's was especially noteworthy: dark, heady fruitcake; homemade marzipan encasing the cake on top and sides with melting richness; sparkling white frosting whipped up into drifts as a foundation for the little Christmas landscape of candy trees with a tiny china reindeer. It was rich and sugary and wonderful; I downed two pieces without the least trouble.

"Tell me, George," I asked, hoping to distract attention from the speed of my fork, "how is your book coming?" George's book was something of a joke in university circles. He'd been writing it forever on some abysmally dull subject. Introducing the topic was risky; it could have kept George going for half an hour at least.

This time he didn't get a chance to get started; Alice, beaming, got in first. "Oh, Dorothy, it's nearly finished, and you haven't heard the real news. We're rather pleased, actually—it's to be published by Oxford University Press! Buried here at Sherebury, George has been rather left out of things, but this may make a difference. Just between us, it will make him a very strong candidate for the Clarendon Chair."

It was my day for inadequate responses. "Er—the Clarendon Chair?"

George condescended to explain. "Of course you've forgotten, Dorothy, you've left the academic world. The Clarendon Chair of History of Holy Scripture, at St. Swithin's College, Oxford. It's vacant just now, and I admit it's rather a plum. I was up for it a good many years ago, but it usually goes to a clergyman. As Alice says, they may make an exception this time. But you know, Alice, we said we wouldn't talk about it yet."

"No, but Dorothy won't tell anyone, I'm sure. She doesn't really know anyone . . ." Alice turned slightly pink and stopped talking.

I was suddenly not hungry anymore. The fact that Alice hadn't intended the slap in the face didn't make it feel any better. George, with his usual tactlessness, had said it baldly: I'd left the academic world. I was a nonperson, in fact. Frank had provided my identity, and now that he was gone . . . I put down my plate and stood up.

"You must forgive me, I have the most terrific headache. Thank you so much for tea, and that sublime cake, Alice, but I must get home. No, George, it's kind of you to offer, but the walk will do me good, I think." George's standard of driving matched his minimal knowledge of cars, and in any case, if I spent any more time with him I was going to break something. "Enjoy the rest of the holidays, and good night."

∞5∞

NIGHT HAD TRULY fallen, though it was just past six. As I groped through the now-dense fog I mused bitterly on its penetrating quality. I was wet to my skin by the time I turned down my street, and very sorry for myself indeed. George and Alice had depressed me, the fog made everything worse, and the sight of my gloomy house—I'd forgotten to leave a light on—was the last straw. It was all very well to make optimistic resolutions when the sun was out, but how did you maintain them in the dismal dark?

Next door a lamp shone warmly through red curtains in the front room, and a gap in the curtains revealed bright flames in a snug little fireplace. On impulse I climbed the steps and knocked.

Jane opened it abruptly, said, "Oh, it's you," and then really looked at me. "Good grief, woman, you're wet through. Come in and have something to warm you."

"Is this a bad time? I was just coming home, and your house looked so friendly . . . but if you're expecting someone, or—"

"No. Wasn't doing anything. Glad to have you." I sighed with relief. Jane almost never bothers to be gracious, but she never tells social lies, either. If she said she was glad to have me, she was.

"All right, now, upstairs with you and we'll get you out of those clothes," she ordered. "My dressing gown is good and warm, and then we'll get some drink into you. Come along, your teeth are chattering."

Jane enjoys old houses, but like Dr. Temple she values comfort and convenience. Her large bathroom, added on long after the house was built, has heated towel racks on which she draped my sweater and slacks while I swathed myself in her brown flannel dressing gown. The kitchen, also added on, also large and well equipped, was beautifully warm, and a potent hot whiskey and water quieted my teeth.

"Went out to tea, did you?" asked Jane.

"Yes, George Chambers invited me over."

She barked a laugh. "Bored you to death about his book, I suppose."

"No, actually it was Alice this time. She seems to think it's going to set the world on fire."

"Doubt it. George may think he's God's gift to scholarship, but the world's not so flammable as all that."

I snickered into my glass, but Jane's face sobered. She studied me over the tops of her steel-rimmed glasses.

"No need to ask if you've heard the news." She ran a hand through her untidy hair.

I nodded. "Last night before I went to bed. But I haven't looked at a paper today. What are they saying?"

"Not much." She shoved over a pile of newsprint. "See for yourself."

I skimmed. The Rev'd Canon Jonathan Billings . . . wound to the head (I shuddered and passed over that one) . . . aged 52 . . . no family living . . . educated Oxford . . . publications *The Roman Occupation and Its Implications*, *Paul and the Young Churches*, *Early Christian Dissent*, etc., etc. . . . . early preferment . . . brilliant career . . . police pursuing vigorously . . .

"It doesn't give much of a picture of the man, does it?" I said finally, shoving the papers back.

She made a sound of disgust. "Makes him sound like some kind of a saint. Which," tossing off her whiskey and pouring a little more, "he was not." She sat back and folded her hands across her stomach.

"I didn't really know him all that well," I said, "but from what's been said, and not said, I get the impression people didn't like him much."

"*Like* him!" The contempt dripped. "One couldn't like the man. He was perfect. Expected everyone else to be perfect. Never lost his temper, just got coldly reasonable, pity you were wrong and too stupid to see it."

"He quarreled with lots of people, then?"

"Didn't 'quarrel' with anyone. Just what I'm saying. Thought it beneath him. Half the town quarreled with *him*."

Jane doesn't suffer fools gladly, but I'd never heard her say anything really scathing before, and I'd never seen her in this combative mood. I glanced at the bottle on the table between us.

"I'm not tipsy," she growled, "though it's not a bad idea. Just bloody furious. The man set the town by its ears when he was alive, made it worse by dying. Going to cause trouble for a lot of innocent people before it's done." She glared at me.

Did I see a glimmer of what was really bothering her? "I wonder," I began tentatively, "if Nigel Evans knows anything about—"

"Who've you been talking to?" Jane demanded fiercely.

"Jane Langland, don't jump on me like that! It's not my fault I stumbled over a body and got mixed up in a murder. Believe me, I'm not enjoying it!"

So I was right. She was silent for a moment, and then made a face.

"Sorry." She moved her glass in little circles on the table. "Didn't intend to lose my temper. Someone's told you Nigel had a row with Billings, I suppose."

I nodded unhappily. "George. Not that I pay much attention to him as a rule . . ."

"Oh, it's true enough. Did he tell you Billings gave him the sack?"

"Oh, no! Not that, too! George overheard them having it out, but he left before the end. His idea was that Nigel was likely to be expelled from the university on the strength of it. But fired! Jane, that's awful! What will he live on? You said he's barely getting along as it is. Although, perhaps, now that . . ."

I stopped and looked at Jane in dawning horror.

"Precisely. You see just how bad it looks. And you're on his side. What will the police think?"

"Half the town had reason to hate him, but Nigel had a large public fight with him the day he died," I recited mechanically. "And lost his job, and might have been expelled from the university. The police are going to jump on it. And you're right, I *am* on his side, though I'm not sure why. I don't even know the kid."

"He's all right, really, as kids go," said Jane, with a show of disinterest that didn't take me in for a moment. "But—it's worse than you know, Dorothy." She took a deep breath, settling her glasses firmly on her nose. "No point in hiding it. He's been in trouble before. Petty stuff—joyriding, the odd small theft. And he's been sent down before. From King's. Cambridge."

"Jane!"

"He can sing. That and first-class A-levels got him a scholarship. But he started a brawl with a policeman and lost everything." She sighed heavily, shaking her head. "The two sides to the Welsh: music and drink."

"He was drunk?"

"I should imagine. Got a temper, yes, but not violent when he's sober. Point is, he'd've had a jolly hard time getting into yet another university. Or finding another post. Properly up against it."

There was a long pause.

"Of course he didn't do it," Jane said in quite an ordinary voice.

"Of course not," I echoed.

"Don't need to be all that polite. No reason why you should believe me, but I know. Spent too long with kids not to know their heads. He's not a killer."

I believed that she believed it. And she does know kids, inside out. But still . . .

"You don't know him all that well; you said so yourself. And George thinks he did it," I pointed out.

"Everyone'll think he did it. Convenient. Poor, not a local, no waves if he's the one." She sighed again. "He's not, though. I know Inga Endicott. Wouldn't have anything to do with him if he were that sort. She's talked to me about him."

Of course. "Well, if you're right, he's in no danger. This is England. Your police—"

She snorted. "Are wonderful. That what you were going to say?"

"Well, compared to the ones in American small towns," I began to reply, defensively.

Jane actually chuckled. "Point taken. Not accusing you of being naive. Police are capable. Also overworked, understaffed, *and* . . . they want a conviction, soon. Canon is an important person, can't mess about with his murder. Have to hope they use sense. Talk to the chief constable."

I was startled. "You want me to talk to Mr. Nesbitt? I'd be glad to, but . . ."

"No, no, sorry, meant *I* must talk to him."

Her telegraphic style had confused me. The rest of her comment went unspoken, but it hung there clearly in the air. What good, after all, could I do? No one would listen to me, the stranger, the nonentity. For all practical purposes, as far as Sherebury was concerned, I didn't exist.

Jane saw the look in my eye, interpreted it correctly,

and changed the subject abruptly. "Dorothy, when are you going to find something to do?"

"To do? About the murder, you mean?"

She gestured impatiently. "About yourself. Need to stop brooding, feeling sorry for yourself. Don't mean to interfere, but it's true, isn't it?"

"I guess so. I mean, yes, of course you're right. I came to the same conclusion this morning. But what is there to do? I can't work, at least I don't think I can, without a permit or something. And who'd hire someone my age, and a foreigner at that?"

"Volunteer. Can't stop you doing that, can they?"

I was in a difficult mood, ready to refuse any constructive suggestions. "Volunteer where? I'm hopeless with flowers, and anyway the cathedral flower guild would freeze me out. They've all lived here since the Ark. I've never done altar guild work, there's no volunteer choir, I don't know anything about the local charities . . ."

"Kids."

". . . I'm no good at collecting money . . . what?"

"You were a teacher. You know how to work with kids. Lots to do, at the cathedral, the university."

"Oh. Well. But they're English kids."

"Kids are kids. And they're not all English. Quite a lot of Americans, Asians, Africans, God knows what." Jane saw the unspoken rebellion in my face. "Now look here. You need a shape to your life. Choose what you want to do yourself, if you don't like my ideas, but do something. Can't just let things close in."

I was startled by the precision of her understanding. One of the unexpected things about widowhood was the way one's world contracted, lost both size and shape. I hadn't helped matters, of course, by moving away from all that was familiar. My life, as Jane had seen, was frighteningly aimless. And hadn't I been telling myself all day that I needed to be more positive?

"I'll think about it, Jane," I hedged. "Meanwhile, do you really believe Nigel is in danger?"

"Don't know. Was hoping he'd come to me for help."

So that was why she was ready for a knock at the door.

"Do what I can, anyway. Probably the only real friend he's got in Sherebury. Except for the Endicotts, if they count. Inga thinks he's all right but irresponsible, parents aren't sure they want their daughter taking up with a young hothead. But I'm too close to it. Police'll question anything I say as partisan." She dismissed it and picked up the bottle. "One more?"

We had one more, and a sandwich, and by that time my clothes had stopped dripping and I could go home to my doubtless furious cat.

As I cut across my back lawn, I nearly had a heart attack when a shadow materialized out of the fog.

"Mrs. Martin." It was a familiar voice. "I'd like to talk to you for a moment, if it's not too much trouble."

I got my breathing back in order and sighed. "Of course, Chief Constable. Come in."

∞6∞

"I DIDN'T MEAN to frighten you," said Mr. Nesbitt, once we'd come through the back door into the kitchen.

"Scared me out of seven years' growth," I said, switching on lights. "May I take your coat? I warn you, though, it's freezing everywhere but in here."

"Thank you, I'll leave it on a chair. I'm sorry about lurking in that melodramatic fashion, but I thought you might not want a police car at your front door, so my driver dropped me off round the corner and I came up the back lane."

"Why, would my neighbors think I was being arrested?" Emmy yowled; I had stepped on her paw as she rubbed my ankle, lobbying about dinner. "Sorry, cat, but it's your own fault. I'm not, am I? Being arrested, I mean? I haven't broken a traffic law in a week or two at least."

He only smiled, and there was an awkward little silence.

"Would you care for a drink?" I said finally in my brightest of voice. "I don't know your rules. *Stop* it, Emmy."

"I'm not strictly on duty," he said gravely, "and I have a driver waiting for me. I'd like a drink, thank you. Whatever you're having."

"I'm having coffee. Jane's been plying me with liquor and coercion. But pour yourself whatever you like, if you don't mind. It's in that cupboard, and the glasses are next to it. I've got to get out of these wet clothes. Emmy, you're just going to have to wait a minute!"

I took a little time over changing, not being at all sure what Nesbitt meant by "not *strictly* on duty." Whatever was coming, I wanted to be prepared. So I dried my hair, hung up all the damp things in the bathroom, got out my favorite red sweater and a pair of slacks that de-emphasized all the reasons I shouldn't wear slacks, and put on fresh makeup. Might as well go in with flags flying.

When I got downstairs Mr. Nesbitt had taken charge. Emmy was purring over a dish of minced turkey, the smell of fresh coffee perfumed the house, and a wood fire crackling on the hearth made my parlor cozy and friendly.

"I hope you don't mind. You did make me free of your kitchen."

"Mind! I'm delighted. Have you eaten, by the way?"

"Yes, thanks, but if you . . ."

"No, Jane fed me. Oh, this coffee is wonderful." I looked at his small glass of what looked liked scotch. "Do you always have to have a chauffeur?"

"Always. I must often take a social drink on various official occasions, and the law—you do know about our drinking and driving laws?"

I nodded. They were extremely strict; I approved even though they cramped my style now that I was alone.

We sipped for a moment in silence. Then I put my cup down and looked at my guest thoughtfully. "Mr. Nesbitt, I don't know a lot about English police procedure, but I do read, and I had the idea chief constables didn't ordinarily go around interrogating witnesses themselves."

"Quite right. Nor do we, ordinarily."

"Well, then? Not that I'm not glad to see you, but . . ."

"But you'd like to know what the hell I'm doing here, making myself at home?"

I laughed, as he had intended. "Something like that."

He put his hands together and studied them for a moment, fingers spread and tips touching in a gesture that made him look more like Alistair Cooke than ever. "I did say I wasn't exactly on duty. This isn't an ordinary case, Mrs. Martin."

"I wish you'd call me Dorothy," I interrupted. "I feel silly sitting here with a man who's just made up my fire and fed my cat, and being all British and formal."

"I *am* British," he pointed out, smiling, "and usually somewhat formal. But I'm delighted. My name is Alan."

"I remember." Did that sound coquettish? Oh, dear. I wanted to be friendly, but not . . . I hurried on. "You were saying?"

"It's not every case, as I'm sure you will realize, in which the chief constable is a witness to the discovery of the body. By rights I suppose I ought to turn the whole thing over to the bloke in the next county and wash my hands of it, except as a minor witness." He ran his hand along the back of his neck. "But it also is not every case in which a high church dignitary is murdered. Sherebury has two poles of influence, as I'm sure you know: the university and the cathedral. Canon Billings was involved in both, as a noted scholar and a clergyman. He was also a very—er—well-known member of the community, sitting on any number of committees and the Borough Council, and so on. If I called this an important murder I'm sure you would misunderstand me. All murders are equally important, but . . . "

"But some are more equal than others. Yes, all right, Emmy, we know you're one of the most equal cats." She settled herself in my lap, motor revving and paws working. "So you've put yourself in charge of this case?"

"Certainly not." He looked almost shocked. "My best

detective chief inspector is in charge, and I may say that I am running the risk of annoying him considerably by butting in. He's an extremely able man, but he has a tendency to be quite intimidating. That's as it should be, of course, but I felt you might be more comfortable talking to someone you knew, at least slightly. Even though my job now is purely administrative, as you've already been over the ground once with me, you won't have to repeat yourself quite so much."

"And if I turn out to be stubborn and uncooperative in a strictly unofficial talk, you can sic him on me."

"Indeed," he said with a small grin.

"Very well." I scratched Emmy's head, and the purr grew even louder. "My will is in order and my prayers are said. Fire away."

There wasn't much to it, after all. He took me through Christmas Eve in agonizing detail, but asked nothing really new. The worst part, describing the appearance of the body, didn't bother me as much as I had expected. Thinking and talking about it had made it seem more and more like something I'd imagined.

"Well, that's that," he said finally. "Nothing terribly helpful, I'm afraid. I'd hoped you might remember noticing something unusual, but I didn't really expect it; it was very dark. There is just one tiny point." He tented his fingers again. "I had the oddest impression at the time that when you realized what you had stumbled over—a body—you were actually relieved. That seemed so peculiar I thought I must be imagining things. But I got the same notion just now when you went through it again."

"Oh." I felt the heat rise to the roots of my hair. "Oh, dear. No, you're not imagining things. But I was."

"Yes?" His eyebrows rose.

"It's going to sound extremely silly," I warned him. "But it was *awfully* dark in there, as you just said. And very quiet, for some reason. Mrs. Allenby said something about the acoustics later. Anyway, it's the oldest part of the church, and—well, I remembered that old story about the ghost. The monk, you know." I stole a glance at him, but his face was politely impassive. "And I got scared," I went on, defiantly. "So I thought I'd open the door, because there's a light outside. Come to think of it, I suppose that one's out from the rewiring, too, but I didn't think of that then. I just wanted some light, so I walked over to the door. And when I stumbled over that bunch of cloth, just for one horrid moment I thought it was a habit, and—" I studied Emmy's back fixedly, fiddling with her ears.

"I'm not going to laugh at you, if that's what you're worried about," said Alan calmly.

"You're not?" I looked up. "Do you believe in ghosts?"

"I don't know that I believe in them. I'm not sure what the phrase means. But I've seen them. I've seen the monk, for that matter. He's not terribly alarming, really." He finished his drink and set down the glass.

I shook my head, to try to clear it. "You're—not at all the way I imagined an English policeman would be."

"Why? Because I trust my own senses? I'd be a poor policeman indeed if I couldn't. At any rate I think I understand your reactions now. A genuine twentieth-century man, even if dead, must have seemed better than a six-teenth-century ghost. More coffee?"

He came back from the kitchen with the pot and another cup and poured some for both of us. "You're feeling a trifle better about it now, aren't you?"

"Is that why you came?" I demanded. "To make sure I wasn't going to have nightmares?"

"One reason," he agreed equably.

"Well, I must say!" I exclaimed indignantly. "I'm perfectly able to take care of myself, you know."

"Of course you are. I'm sure you also look after your friends when they need a bit of help. Why should you resent it when your friends do the same for you?"

"Well—when you put it that way—" I sipped my coffee. "I suppose Jane sent you."

"Do you expect me to answer that?"

"Probably not. Will you answer something else?"

"Depends what it is."

"All right, you've been asking me questions. It's my turn. What makes the police so sure it was murder? I thought it was an accident, that he somehow managed to drop that candlestick on his head, or something. And you did, too, that night."

"Let's say"—he got up to stir the fire—"let's say I reserved judgment. Even then, there were some things that weren't quite consistent. As to our suspicions— you're not by any conceivable stretch of the imagination a suspect, so I suppose there's no real reason you shouldn't know, if I can trust you not to tell anyone. Anyone, you understand."

I nodded.

"There are two things." He stood by the mantel and ticked them off on his large hands. "First, Canon Billings did not die where he was found. There are various indications—"

"Marks on the body, hypostasis—is that how you pronounce it, when the blood pools in the part of the body that was lowest?"

His expression was really rather funny. If he had been any less polite, it would have been an openmouthed stare.

"Don't look at me like that. I told you I read. Mysteries. Lots of them. What was the other thing?"

He sat down again. "Since you're such an expert, supposing you tell me."

"Sarcasm is the tool of the devil, one of my friends used to say. I expect you're worried about the weapon. Not the candlestick. Wrong shape, doesn't fit the wound. Right?"

"Right. Am I going to have to revise my opinion about you as a suspect?"

I looked at him sharply, but his expression was entirely amiable, so far as I could tell. "No, I didn't kill the man, although from what Jane tells me, I was one of the few people in Sherebury who never wanted to. She sounds as if she'd like to award a medal to whoever did it."

"And can you tell me who that might be, while you're busy deducing?"

"Jane thinks . . . but I really have no idea. None." I closed my mouth firmly, although of course the horse was already well out of the barn.

"Ah, and what does Jane think? She's an astute lady, as her burglary incident gave me good reason to know. I'd be very interested."

I found it hard to meet his keen eye. "She doesn't know either."

He just looked at me, benignly.

"Oh, all right, you'd think I'd have learned to keep my mouth shut at my age. Jane thinks you're likely to suspect . . . someone she's sure didn't do it. And if you want to know any more you're going to have to ask her. I won't say another word."

"I see." He looked at me with no trace of a smile, now, on his face. "Mrs.—Dorothy. I do hope you fully realize what it is you're involved in."

"What do you mean?"

"Only that this isn't a trivial matter. I understand your instinct to shield the innocent. Very laudable. But murderers are dangerous. It's amazing how people forget that basic fact. It doesn't do to protect a murderer, even when you're sure you have the best of motives. If young Nigel Evans—oh, it's easy enough to see who you're talking about—if he killed Canon Billings, he's a ruthless young thug who doesn't deserve your sympathy, or Jane's, for one moment."

There was a little silence. "And if he didn't?" I finally murmured.

"Then he has nothing to worry about. We're not infalli-
ble, Dorothy, but we make very few mistakes with this
sort of thing. But please don't lose sight of the essential
point. Which is that, as the finder of the body, you could
be in danger."

"But I don't know anything I haven't told you, believe
me."

"I know that. But does the murderer? You see, whoever he is, or she, of course—may I stick to one pronoun
for simplicity?—he's not in his right mind just now. I
don't mean he's certifiably mad, simply that when a person murders, for whatever immediate cause, it boils
down to one reason in the end: He thinks there is no other
choice. He's in a corner with only one way out. Then, once
he's done it, he finds himself in another corner, being
pushed even harder. And anyone who has no options left
is dangerous, because it doesn't matter what he does—he
thinks nothing can make things worse. Desperation used
to be viewed as the ultimate sin, you know. I'm not sure
there isn't something in that, if only because of what a
desperate person can do."

"Here endeth the lesson?" I said a trifle shakily, after a
pause.

Either that piece of flippancy irritated him, or else he
was embarrassed. Or perhaps he had accomplished what
he came for and was tired of my company. At any rate he
stood up and began to shrug into his coat. "Quite right. I
should leave the preaching to the parsons." He put out
his hand and shook mine, formally. "Thank you for far
more time than I intended to take, Dorothy. Good night.
Lock your door."

With that he was gone. I obediently locked the door,
feeling a little blank. The cathedral clock struck the nine
strokes of the hour, sounding, to my overheated imagination, a little like a knell.

✌7✍

"MY TEXT IS taken from the thirteenth chapter of St. Paul's first letter to the Corinthians: 'Though I speak with the tongues of men and of angels, and have not charity, I am become as sounding brass or a tinkling cymbal. . . . Charity suffereth long, and is kind; charity envieth not; charity vaunteth not itself, is not puffed up. Doth not behave itself unseemly, seeketh not her own, is not easily provoked, thinketh no evil; Rejoiceth not in iniquity, but rejoiceth in the truth; Beareth all things, believeth all things, hopeth all things, endureth all things. . . . And now abideth these three, faith, hope, and charity; but the greatest of these is charity.'"

Sunday morning, the ten o'clock Eucharist. Only two days after Christmas, and the congregation had dropped to normal levels, fitting comfortably into the choir. The clergy, I thought, must find the contrast depressing. Certainly the dean, standing at the brass lectern, looked far from happy, though goodness knows there were plenty of other reasons for distress. The poor man seemed to have lost both height and weight, and there were pouches under his eyes. I settled myself for his sermon.

"St. Paul's essay on love is one of the most familiar and most beloved passages from all his writings. Although I have given you a longer text than usual, I have not quoted the essay in full, as many of you know; in fact, I daresay many of you know the entire chapter by heart.

"But do you, indeed? You know the words, but have you taken to your hearts their meaning? Dearly beloved, there is in this small community, perhaps in this very cathedral parish, at least one who has not. We pray in the Litany to be delivered from 'envy, hatred, malice, and all uncharitableness.' Here among us these dreadful sins have struck with dreadful force in the sin and crime of murder."

The word hung there in a dead silence. The usual rustles stopped; for a moment no one seemed to breathe.

For many of us it wasn't entirely unexpected. The dean was not a man to ignore the disagreeable or try to paper it over. The tourists here and there, however, looked as if they were getting a good deal more than they'd bargained for. We were all in for an uncomfortable interval, certainly. Would it be, for one among us, much worse than that?

I hastily dismissed that speculation and concentrated firmly on the dean, who leaned earnestly over the lectern.

"It had been my intention to speak to you this morning, as I always do at this time of the year, about the glory of this Christmas season and the wonder that we celebrate each December. And indeed we must not lose sight of that glory, that wonder, in the midst of our great trouble. But the terrible event that has befallen us has made it necessary that I depart from the seasonal and speak for a little of more somber things. It is not my business here to deal with the fact of murder. That is terrible enough. It is a frightening, a devastating thought, that a canon of this cathedral could be struck down in his own church. But many of us have been thinking of this horror and little else, I suspect, for two days, and it is no intent of mine to dwell on it. I urge you, rather, to think about the sins in each one of us that, unchecked, can lead to such an act as murder. We may never know precisely why Canon Billings died. But we can think about the two powerful and terrible sins that certainly led to the act, and that tempt all of us: the sins of pride and despair."

I was startled to hear the chief constable's thoughts in the mouth of the dean; my nerves tightened another notch.

"You might think at first that these two sins have little to do with one another, that, indeed, they are directly opposed. Surely pride is an exaggerated idea of one's own importance and powers, while despair is the feeling of powerlessness, the notion that one can do nothing about a terrible problem. But they have their root in a common idea, the idea that one's own goals and aims and desires come first. All murderers, I am told by the experts, have one common motivation, no matter how complex the issues may seem: They want something, and some person stands between them and their desire, so that person must be removed."

The dean took off his glasses and continued with slow emphasis, looking searchingly at his congregation as he spoke.

"You may be saying to yourselves, as I have said to myself, that you would never harbor the idea of taking a life, and I hope and trust that we tell ourselves the truth. But do you not see that the lack of charity, in Paul's sense, the lack of long-suffering and hope and endurance, and the presence of charity's opposites, conceit, envy, self-seeking, are what lead to the valuation of self over others—indeed, the love of self more than God? The moment you decide your goals are more important than your neighbor's, and his must therefore give way, you have taken the first step on a road that may lead to destruction."

Whew! One could almost hear the low whistles; certainly

a brow here and there was being mopped. Did everyone
else feel as irrationally guilty as I did? I was in a good
position to watch reactions to this strong stuff, but they
weren't informative. I didn't see Nigel anywhere. Jane, sitting surrounded by her kids, appeared to be thinking
about something else. George Chambers, typically, wasn't
there; Alice's face was set in that expressionless mask the
well-bred English find so useful for hiding feelings. So
were most of the others I could see. If the mask had stiff-
ened into anything more sinister in any particular case, I
couldn't tell. The tourists' eyes were fixed firmly on the
fan vaulting and their minds, I suspected, just as firmly
removed from the scene.

My own mind wandered as the familiar words of St.
Paul echoed through it. I could hear the rest of the chapter, too . . . *for now we see through a glass, darkly* . . . if there
was ever a description of my state of mind, that was it. A
lot of his words fit, in fact, as a description of what I
should be and wasn't. I was certainly not long-suffering. I
was very easily provoked indeed, and ready to endure
very little. Puffed up, well . . . I had a sudden vision of
George's face, literally puffed up and purple as he went
on and on about Nigel. Oh, Paul knew what he was talking about, all right, when it came to human nature. I
sighed, resettled my hat, and tried once more to listen.
The dean had veered aside from his theme to a discourse
about Paul himself.

"He was, of course, a masterful man, and one whose
past life left him with no illusions about sin. And the
church at Corinth gave him great cause for concern. The
epistles we so value today are, we think, but a small sample of the chiding letters he so often had to write as he
moved about the Mediterranean, hearing news in one
place or another about the new churches he had left
behind."

I remembered I had been told in a long-ago Sunday-school class that there was probably a third letter to the Corinthians in the New Testament for the first few centuries, but that it had been lost or stolen or suppressed or something. Where was it? I wondered. Had it ever really existed? Speculating, I missed most of the dean's observations about the young churches, but I surfaced again at the sound of a familiar name.

". . . Canon Billings, whose memorial service will be held on Tuesday at two o'clock. I bid your prayers for him.

"And now unto God the Father, God the Son, and God the Holy Ghost, be ascribed all might and power, all dominion and majesty, world without end, amen."

I followed the rest of the service mechanically. I do like to be challenged and stimulated from the pulpit, but there was such a thing as *too* topical a message. I had come to church hoping for a healthy dose of serenity and reassurance, but even here, the world had nosed its ugly way in. Oh, well, religion was never meant to be an escape from life, just a way of dealing with it.

Mr. Wallingford, I noticed with amusement and some exasperation, was making the most of the situation. His shocked, mournful gaze as he took up the collection shook loose from the tourists a good deal of folding money. With the smallest bank note at five pounds these days, the take must have been considerable. How upset the dean would be if he realized the way the verger was using the tragedy!

It was a little odd, come to think of it, that Mr. Wallingford was presiding. The main service of a Sunday was Mr. Swansworthy's responsibility as head verger. But he was inclined to dyspepsia; perhaps he'd had too much Christmas. Certainly Wallingford was glorying in his importance. I watched him strut to the altar rail with the collection and was vividly reminded of the money changers in the temple.

Tea and coffee are served in the old scriptorium after
the major Sunday services. As I stood at the end of the
serving line I found myself next to Jeremy Sayers, the
organist/choirmaster, whom I had met once or twice.
"Lovely service, Mr. Sayers. The choir was marvelous, as
always."

He bowed slightly, graciously, his fair hair falling into
his eyes. "Madam. The sermon was a bit disconcerting,
however, don't you think? I very nearly stood up and
shouted that I had done it. I've always had a suggestible
nature, you know. And there was something in all that
guilt hanging about in the air . . ."

"Well, they do say confession is good for the soul, but
in this case perhaps you were wise to forbear," I replied
in the same spirit. Conversation with this man, I remembered, had a tendency to wander off into fantasy.

"You have *no* idea," he continued as we reached the
serving table, "how truly delighted I am that the man is
safely dead. I shall play that memorial service next week
with the greatest glee, I can't *tell* you. Coffee?"

"Tea, thanks, if there's any without milk."

"From the look of it," he said, surveying suspiciously
the cups full of dubious liquid, "you'd be safer with all
the additives possible. However, it's your digestion."

I found a table in the corner with the last two empty
chairs in the room. "Shall we sit here? There's one bun
left, do you want to split it?"

He shuddered, holding up crossed hands in the manner of one warding off vampires as he slid his slender
form onto the chair.

"So I gather you didn't like Canon Billings?" I said
through a mouthful of slightly stale pastry.

"I doubt," he said, dramatically dropping his voice
half an octave, "there are three people who liked him in
Sherebury. In England. In the universe. 'I did not love
thee, Dr. Fell,' but the reason why I know perfectly well."

"Why?" I asked, and held my breath. There was no reason on earth why he should answer.

Mr. Sayers, however, seemed perfectly willing to talk about it. "My dear Mrs. Martin, you are surely the only person in the parish who doesn't know that the canon hated my music. He was hell-bent on getting me sacked."

"Not you, too?" I said, startled, but Sayers wasn't paying attention.

"Too modern, you see. The only proper church music, in the mind of our ancient scholar, was modal and monophonic. Gregorian chant was the epitome. Polyphony verged on the sacrilegious and Bach was *entirely* over the top. He actually used to quote a monk about how music used to be simple and manly, and modern works were 'lascivious beyond measure.' Isn't it marvelous? The monk in question lived in the fourteenth century." He moved his glasses back on his bony nose and studied my reaction.

"Good grief, you're serious, aren't you?"

"I exaggerate a trifle. But only a trifle, I do assure you. And as he and I are—were—the only ones on the cathedral staff with the *remotest* knowledge of music, he stood a good chance of getting his point across to the Dean and Chapter."

"The dean would never have agreed to outlaw Bach!" I was scandalized. "Mr. Allenby may not be terribly musical, but he has good sense. What about hymns?"

"I did say I was exaggerating. Bach would probably have survived, although I give you my *solemn* word our Jonathan thought him too romantic and thrilling. But in any case the canon didn't deal in actual dates and composers, you see. Of course not. He made statements about modern music being difficult, a trifle 'advanced' for our congregation, perhaps not conducive to a spirit of reverence, and they all agreed. The hitch was, they thought he was talking about 1970 music when he really meant 1770, or thereabouts. He'd have got me out in the end, and a man of his own in, who'd have done as Billings liked. So you *can* see why I'm not wearing a black veil."

"I can see why you had an excellent reason for wishing Mr. Billings well away from here," I said lightly.

"Oh, but not the *best* reason," said Mr. Sayers with a bright little laugh, tilting his head to one side. "Oh, dear me, no. Ask someone about the verger who was dipping into the till." He looked at his cup with loathing. "I wonder someone didn't simply poison our canon's coffee one morning after Matins. He'd never have noticed the taste. Now, my dear, duty calls; no rest for the wicked. Ta-ta."

Well! One tiny prod at a rock, and look how much had crawled out! I wondered if it was all spite, or if there was any truth in it. That crack about the verger . . .

"Morning, Dorothy." Jane, who had been presiding at one of the tea urns, was now free to enjoy her own cuppa. She dropped into the folding chair with a grunt.

"Hello. I was just going to find you. I've been listening to gossip and I have to tell you . . ." I lowered my voice. "Did you know the choirmaster was about to be fired on account of Billings, and one of the vergers was in trouble over theft? I don't suppose you know which one?"

"Wallingford," she answered promptly. "Discovered some way to steal from the collection. Everyone knows, but there's no proof. Billings was hot on the trail."

"But—if everyone knows, why haven't the police done anything about it? I mean, that's surely the best motive."

"I told you. There's no proof. Have to have proof. That's why they've arrested Nigel."

I looked at her, dumb. She was in perfect control of herself, but her style became even more telegraphic than usual.

"Won't stick. No real evidence. Trying to scare him into confession. Won't do it."

"You think they'll release him, then?" I said, swallowing and trying to match her composure.

"Bound to. Soon. He'll come to me, most likely. His landlady won't keep him, now. Best be getting home. Cheerio." She patted me on the arm, gave a reasonably good imitation of a smile, and strode off, back straight and shoulders set. Boadicea must have looked just like her, going into battle against the Romans.

Admirable, but it had been an unsuccessful battle.

Left alone, I started chasing stray ideas like a squirrel in a cage. What if Nigel was indeed a murderer? But his motive seemed entirely inadequate, and Jane claimed he just wasn't that kind of person. I was much happier with the idea of Wallingford as villain. But that was only, I chided myself, because I disliked him heartily. And how awful to think someone a murderer just because he was rude.

Not that Jeremy Sayers was exactly polite or charming. But he was at least entertaining, and a glorious musician. I didn't want it to be him, either. Oh, I didn't want it to be anybody I knew.

As I tried to organize my thoughts, I found myself walking back into the cathedral. And that was as it should be, I thought. Here in this place was somehow the heart of the problem. And here was also the serenity I needed.

The choir was practicing for Evensong, sending soothing, muted echoes into the nave. I wandered aimlessly, absorbing the deep, enduring peace, admiring the pools of colored light on the gray stone floor, letting my eye be carried up toward the incomparable roof.

And suddenly stopped dead still, my heart thumping erratically. From a clerestory arch, a figure looked down at me. By the light of the great chandeliers, restored to electricity now that Christmas Eve was over, the figure was unmistakable for a moment, until it glided silently into the shadows. Cowled and hooded, gowned in a long robe tied with rope. A faceless, noiseless monk.

❧ 8 ❧

AS I SAT watching the dull winter landscape move past the grimy window of the train, I tried to think coherently about my situation, ghost and all.

Monday morning having arrived, I had decided to go up to London as planned, though I had trouble mustering any enthusiasm for shopping. Nigel had been released Sunday afternoon, as predicted, and had sought refuge with Jane, also as predicted. She was fully occupied in looking after his creature comforts, and was herself finding considerable comfort in the effort, I noticed. There was nothing useful I could do for either of them at the moment, so off I went. Perhaps I could bring a fresh mind back to Sherebury.

Right now my mind didn't want to function at all. It was that kind of day. The varieties of revolting weather England could produce, I thought drearily, were limitless. Yesterday's brilliant sunshine had been replaced by dismal clouds, not at the moment producing rain, but continuing to threaten. The fields with their hedgerows looked dirty and bleak; the sheep, usually charming in their cotton-ball silliness, were dingy.

The wheels clacked out their monotonous rhythm. Think. I should think. My eyelids drooped; my head nodded. I jerked it up. Someone murdered the canon. Nigel, the choirmaster, the verger. Verger. Verging on disaster. Master the disaster. Choirmaster ordered a cannon for the "1812 Overture." Kill the canon with a cannon. Give that man a medal, he killed the canon. Twenty-one-gun salute . . .

The train boomed its way into a tunnel and I woke abruptly, the entangled images of my dream still filling my head. Odd, I thought, that the ghost had played no part in the web my unconscious mind had spun. Did that mean he was irrelevant?

Or nonexistent, a corner of my mind whispered.

At that, however, I shook my head firmly, causing my flowery hat to wobble. The guard, passing through to punch tickets, stared and forgot about my ticket entirely. It was an especially nice hat, a sort of Queen Mum affair in lavender with tiny felt violets all over it. I smiled brightly at the guard, settled the hat more securely, and got back to my thoughts. No, the ghost was real. I knew what I had seen. Either he had nothing to do with the murder, or my subconscious didn't know what it was talking about.

It was time, my schoolteacher voice said firmly, to get my thoughts in order. And that meant putting them down on paper; I'm a confirmed list maker. I pulled a pad and pen out of my purse and set to work briskly.

Under the heading "Suspects," I listed Nigel Evans, Jeremy Sayers, choirmaster, and Robert Wallingford, verger.

If my sources were right, there were lots more, virtually everyone who knew the man, in fact, but these three would do for a start. I went back to the list, noting things of importance under each name.

Nigel Evans. George thinks he did it. Jane says he didn't. Don't know him at all myself. Had good reason to dislike Billings, and to fear him, and they were witnessed in a violent quarrel.

*Jeremy Sayers. Don't know him well. Fine musician.
Difficult personality, caustic tongue. Admits he had an excellent reason to kill Billings. Maybe hatred as well as fear of losing job? N.B.: Would he tell me all that if there were really
anything to it?*

*Robert Wallingford. If rumors are true, best motive so far.
Not only would have lost job if Billings found proof of stealing,
but would face criminal prosecution. Not a young man, might
be desperate.*

The refreshment trolley passed and I bought a cup of
tepid coffee, took a few sips, and turned back to my list.
Not a terribly inspired document, I decided. It did look as
if Billings had specialized in raising the unemployment
rate, but that was the only pattern I could find. And most
of what I had written was hearsay, not evidence. I turned
to a fresh page and headed it "Action."

*Find out if choirmaster really might have lost job. Talk to
dean? Check whereabouts on Christmas Eve. Find out about
verger rumors. (Dean again? Not likely. Who?) Ditto whereabouts. Meet Nigel, size him up. Ditto whereabouts. Query:
Was Billings going to fire anyone else?*

And what, if anything, does the ghost have to do with
it? I decided not to commit that to paper.

The easiest items to check were those whereabouts.
That's why the police had almost certainly already done
so. I was sure that was why they'd let Nigel go; he must
have been able to prove he was someplace innocent during the relevant time. Or at least his story must have been
convincing enough to create a reasonable doubt.

The trouble with my other two suspects was, of course,
that Sayers and Wallingford were probably exactly where
they should have been on Christmas Eve, in and around
the cathedral, which still left them with ample opportunity to take a little break and bash the canon on the head.
He might actually have been killed in some place that
could implicate the murderer—the verger's office, say, or

the organ loft—which would explain why the body had been moved. What on earth could I do about *that*, look for bloodstains? I wouldn't know a bloodstain if it appeared on my kitchen floor; besides, the police were surely doing all that.

In fact, the police were doing everything that needed to be done, and I knew it perfectly well. I was simply— what? Playing cops and murderers? No, conducting an exercise in logic, my mind replied with dignity.

Then what about the ghost, said the skeptical voice. Where's your logic with him?

I considered. I didn't really believe in him—did I? But if not a ghost, then someone was playing games in the cathedral, and why? I sighed loudly and crossed out both pages.

If my list had no other virtues, it had occupied me into town; the train was pulling into Victoria Station. I stuffed notebook and pen back into purse, put on coat and reset-tled hat as I walked down the aisle, darted back to get my umbrella, and stepped out into the glorious bustle of London.

I wouldn't want to live in London. It's dirty and wildly expensive, and all those people in a perpetual hurry are wearying after a while. But for a day or two I find it enormously exhilarating to be a part of that vast stream of humanity, treading the streets that Dickens once trod, and Churchill and Shakespeare and Christie and Sayers and Elizabeth I and almost everyone I admire. I love the Houses of Parliament and the fish-and-chip shops, the flower stalls and Piccadilly Circus, even the smell of the double-decker red buses. Inhaling a deep breath of London, I plunged into the horde battling its way toward the Underground.

When I surfaced again at Knightsbridge the rain was pelting down. Umbrella firmly clutched, I made a run for Harrod's, getting there just as the doors opened and hundreds of bargain hunters surged inside. Gird your loins, Dorothy, this is the world of The Christmas Sales!

Three hours later I emerged in my usual post-shopping condition: exhausted, heavily laden, extremely pleased with several bargains, already beginning to wonder what on earth I was going to do with two or three impulsive purchases, and ravenous. No point in trying to get into any of Harrod's own restaurants; they were as crowded as the rest of the store. No, I had a much better idea: pub lunch!

And I knew just the pub. The Museum Tavern, across the street from the British Museum. Good, cheap food, good beer, and after I was rested and refreshed I could wander over to explore the BM for a while before tea. It was a straight shot by Underground, but with parcels to carry I was going to indulge in a taxi. One of England's finest contributions to civilization, the London taxi is as big as a parlor, and as comfortable. Or maybe I feel that way because I allow myself the luxury only when I'm too tired to walk.

At lunch I confined myself to beer and a salad, mindful of a luxurious tea to come. The pub wasn't crowded, fickle London apparently preferring, today, the exotic delights of commerce to the esoteric ones of learning, so I took time to inventory my purchases. I'd paid too much for the suit and the electric blanket, but the black hat was a bargain—smart, but not too conspicuous for the funeral tomorrow.

I didn't have to think about that now. As for the earrings and the calendar and the teapot, if I didn't like them when I got them home, I could always give them away. And I had, at last, bought a large box of Christmas crackers. Not Harrod's best, but good ones; they'd be fun next year.

If I were still here next year.

I didn't need to pursue that thought, either. Gathering

up my parcels with some difficulty, I staggered across the street to the museum.

"Not got a bomb in any of that lot, 'ave you, madam?" asked the cloakroom attendant with a broad accent and a broader wink. Apparently I didn't look much like a terrorist.

"I don't think they sell bombs at Harrod's," I replied gravely, "although I'm not sure, they have everything else."

He ran his scanner across the bags rather casually and stowed them away, and relieved of my burden I wandered happily. I went first to greet old friends, the Elgin Marbles, the Portland Vase, the Rosetta Stone. I was caught and held once more, as I always am, by that relatively small piece of stone whose inscription, repeated in Greek, demotic Egyptian, and hieroglyphs, gave scholars the key to ancient Egyptian language and civilization. Such an unassuming little rock to mean so much. Imagine finding it—soldiers are tearing down a wall when they see that one of the stones has writing on it. An officer sees it—but that is Greek! He knows Greek . . . what if the other two languages repeat the same message? Could be interesting, important even. He calls other officers; work comes to a stop as they excitedly pore over the Greek and speculate. . . .

How lucky they had some idea what they had found. It could have been broken up for gravel. I shivered, wondering how much the world had lost through carelessness, or, worse, sloppy scholarship.

After a while I headed for the Egyptian rooms and browsed among the antiquities there, marveling once more at the preservation of artifacts so many hundreds and thousands of years old. Moving from the mummies, which have always held me in a kind of horrified fascination, to the papyri, I was studying one dimly lit display case when a hand on my shoulder made me jump a foot.

"Dorothy Martin, for pete's sake. How *are* you? Haven't seen you for ages. What are you doing here? Oh, sorry, did I scare you?"

"Startled me, that's all, Charles." I exhaled and removed my hand from my heart, whose efforts to leap out of my chest were slowing down. "I was a couple of millennia away; thought you were a mummy come to life. How lovely to see you! I'm up for the sales, but I got tired of bargains and came here for a breather. What are you doing out of your cell?"

For Charles Lambert, an archivist from Frank's university in Hillsburg, was researching ancient manuscripts in England, and spent a good deal of his time in a tiny carrel lent him by the museum.

"Oh, I come up for air every now and then. I'm headed for some coffee. Want some?"

"I'm having tea in an hour or so, but I'd love to sit down and talk. You know, the rest of me doesn't seem so old, but my feet are about eighty-five."

"So what's going on in your part of the world? I haven't been there for ages," said Charles when we had found a table in the coffee shop. "Nothing exciting, I'll bet. The charm of a little backwater like Sherebury is that nothing ever happens."

"No, nothing much," I agreed. "Except battle and murder and sudden death."

"Say what?" He blinked.

"Sorry, I was quoting the *Book of Common Prayer*. Apparently you don't read the papers, Charles. We've had a spectacular murder, hadn't you heard?"

"Are you kidding?"

"I wish I were. I'm trying to be flippant about it because I'm involved, in a way, and it's actually rather horrid. A canon of the cathedral was murdered, and I found the body. You can see why I'm past being scared by you."

"Good Lord, that's terrible! Who killed him, and why?"

"That's just what nobody knows, you see. I'm concerned about it, not only because of finding him, but because one of Jane Langland's young friends seems to be the chief suspect. You remember Jane?"

"No one who's met Jane could ever forget her. Who's the kid?"

"A boy named Nigel Evans. Jane is sure he had nothing to do with it, and she's probably right, but it's certain that Nigel hated the canon. In which, I may say, he was not alone. Jonathan Billings had a real talent for making enemies."

"Billings! Do you mean to say that's who got killed? But I know him! I saw him just the other day, here."

"Here! What was he doing here?"

"I don't know for sure, and I wondered about it at the time. See, I met him when I was in Sherebury that time— you remember—working in the cathedral library."

"Of course. I'd forgotten. Doing something about medieval manuscripts, weren't you?"

"And old Billings didn't make it any easier, let me tell you. He has—had—that good old librarian's idea that all the books ought to be left nice and safe on the shelves. It took the dean to finally convince him I really did need to see some of the stuff. Anyway, I ran into him, oh, a month or so ago, I guess, in the Reading Room. He wanted a book I was using, and he got downright nasty about it. Said he was just in London for the day, whereas I could get it anytime. *Implied* that he was English and I was a damned foreigner and he had a better right to it than I did."

I sighed. "That sounds like him, all right. Arrogant, demanding, rude. What a description of a priest!"

"He must have made one hell of a lousy priest, but I've got to hand it to the guy; he *was* a scholar. But listen,

Dorothy, he was up to something that day. I don't know what. He usually came straight to the point, but this time he was cagey. As if he wanted to ask me something, but didn't want me to know what he was after."

"For heaven's sake, what did he say?"

"Well, he marched over to my reading desk and said he needed the book. Just like that, no please, or excuse me for interrupting, just 'I need to use that book for an hour.' And I said I was in the middle of something and wouldn't be finished until late afternoon, and he argued for a while until an attendant shut him up. And then he got polite—for him—and asked me what I was working on, and if the book helped, and like that. Just small talk, see, but he kept looking at the book as if he wanted to grab it out of my hands. And finally he left."

"Well, that doesn't make much sense. I suppose he was working on some new project."

"Oh, yeah, he mentioned his latest book. He didn't say what it was about, though."

"I know he just got back from a trip—to Greece, I think. I never really paid any attention to the man, except that on the rare occasions I went into the cathedral library, it was pleasanter if he wasn't around. I'm afraid he won't be a great loss, poor man."

"To scholarship, he will. He knew his stuff. Not my period, really, first century, but he was good. Pity."

The real pity was that the only good word anyone had found to say about him was so dry and academic. Perhaps it would count at the Pearly Gates, though. I hoped.

I was more than ready for my tea when my taxi dropped me at the Ritz. One look at the Palm Court banished both exhaustion and the shade of Canon Billings. That bastion of luxury and elegance was all it had ever been, a glorious Edwardian nonsense in pink and green and gold. Lynn and Tom were waiting at the table to which I was escorted with as much ceremony as if I were a duchess, many of whom, I had no doubt, had occupied that same elegant little pink velvet chair. Could the service have had something to do with my hat?

Tom gazed at it in a state of shock, and Lynn grinned broadly but forebore to comment. "We ordered for you, Dorothy. We knew you'd be tired and hungry. Indian all right, I hope?"

The Indian tea was more than all right. It was ambrosial. Without apology, and with very little conversation, I worked my way through six different kinds of sandwiches, scones with strawberry jam and cream, and several cups of tea. When I had made choices from the bountiful pastry tray and polished off the confections, I felt as sated and content as Esmeralda after her turkey. I stretched myself in my chair with a sigh of utter fulfillment.

"You saved my life, I think. That was elegant, thank you very much indeed."

"Had a tough couple of days, have you, D.?" asked Tom, who had offered a few desultory remarks while I gorged myself, but had tactfully stayed off the subject of Sherebury.

"Moderately. Not too bad, I guess, considering. I *am* getting tired of being haunted by Jonathan Billings, though. I even ran into him in the British Museum, figuratively speaking." I related my encounter.

"Funny," commented Tom. "Funny man in a lot of ways, I hear. Well, if things get too much for you down there in the boonies, you can always come up and stay with us for a while."

"I'll remember that," I said with real gratitude. "This has been wonderful, you two, but I've got a train to catch. Remind me that I owe you one."

I intended to do some more hard thinking on the way back, but British Rail had, from its somewhat decrepit collection of rolling stock, provided one of the

old compartment-style coaches for the train home. I
made for it like a homing pigeon, and five minutes out of
Victoria I was asleep. I would have slept right past my
station if the guard hadn't remembered my hat from the
morning and wakened me. There are some advantages to
being conspicuous.

∽9∾

TUESDAY MORNING. Dark, damp, dismal. The rain had turned once more to thick fog that blanketed the town, condensing on every surface and dripping steadily from every gray twig. It had crept into my old house through all the chinks and settled in a fine mist on everything I touched, including the cat. Emmy was as irritable as I. No cat likes to be wet, and her attempts to lick the moisture from her fur simply made matters worse. Naturally it was all my fault. In the delicately balanced relationship of feline and human, there is one basic assumption: When anything is amiss, from insufficient food to disagreeable weather to the annoying behavior of another cat, the human is to blame. Conversely, when life is good, when peace, harmony, and warmth prevail, the cat's smug look will tell you who gets the credit. Of course.

She gave me no peace until she got me to turn on the electric heater in the parlor, then ignored it completely, stalked into the kitchen, and commented crossly on my procrastination in the matter of breakfast.

"I should like to point out, Esmeralda, madam," I said with some asperity (after preparing her food), "that there are people in this world who prefer dogs to cats. Dogs, who offer uncritical adoration at all times. Dogs, who do

as they are told and don't change their minds every five
minutes. How would you like a dog in this house?"

Esmeralda turned away from her dish, gave me a long,
thoughtful look, rolled onto the base of her spine with
one rear leg pointing skyward, and began attending to
matters of personal hygiene. Sufficient comment.

I brewed myself tea, letting it get cold while I over-
cooked an egg and burned some toast. After toying with
the unappetizing mess for a few minutes, telling myself it
was terrible to waste food, I gave up and dumped it all
into the sink. The truth was, I finally admitted to myself,
neither the weather nor the cat nor an inedible breakfast
was at the heart of my bad temper. It was the memorial
service.

I absolutely did not want to go to Canon Billings's
memorial service this afternoon. I've always hated funerals, whatever they're called, with an unreasoning passion.
When I've been close to the person who died, or to the
family, it's all I can do not to make a fool of myself, so I sit
there with clenched teeth getting a dreadful headache
from suppressed tears. I can never think of the right thing
to say to the family; in fact I usually can't say anything at
all over the lump in my throat. When I *haven't* liked the
person it's worse. I sit, then, thinking of the waste, wishing I could have been nicer while they were alive. Of
course, ever since . . . well, the last few months, all funerals had reminded me of . . . anyway, I didn't want to go.

I had to go.

I didn't need to let it spoil the whole day, however,
reminding myself of my resolution to be positive. Why
didn't I go over and talk to Jane? My curiosity about
Charles Lambert's odd conversation with Billings at the
BM demanded satisfaction. Maybe Jane would know
what the canon had been working on before he died.
And—oh, inspiration!—I could take Jane that teapot I was
definitely having second thoughts about. Besides, she had

central heating, and made an awfully good breakfast when she was in the mood.

I refused to put on anything subdued. Time enough for that later. Red. Red sweater and a Royal Stewart kilt I had bought in an unwise moment. It did nothing at all for my figure, but a great deal for my morale. And that hat crocheted out of bits and pieces of brilliantly colored yarn. So there!

"Dorothy. Good to see you. Come in. Cup of tea?"

"Here, I even brought you something to make it in. A Harrod's bargain."

"Hmmm." Jane held it at arm's length to get a good look through the bottom of her bifocals, then looked at me appraisingly over the top of them. We both burst out laughing.

"Oh, goodness, you're right, it really is awful, isn't it? All those roses . . . here, I'll take it back."

"You will not," she said firmly. "A gift is a gift. Perfect for the jumble sale in February." She put it on the hall table and closed the door on the fog. "Had any breakfast? Just getting around to it ourselves."

Ourselves? Oh, yes, Nigel. I'd actually forgotten about him, and I found myself ambivalent about meeting him. Although I wanted to make my own judgment about his character, nothing I'd heard indicated he'd be a comfortable companion at the breakfast table, or anywhere else, for that matter. "Oh, I don't want to intrude," I temporized.

"Nonsense." Jane snorted with a sound exactly like a horse. "Bacon or sausage? Or both?"

"Whatever you're having." I followed her meekly into the kitchen, expecting to find Nigel but seeing only assorted dogs noisily finishing their meal. Jane, too, has her priorities straight: Feed the animals first.

"How is Nigel?" And where is he, but I didn't ask.

"Well enough. Bit depressed. Went out to fetch a bottle of milk."

"Jane, he won't want me here, he'll be feeling touchy about strangers. I'd better . . ."

"Afraid of him, Dorothy? He didn't murder anybody, you know." She was placidly assembling eggs, meat, butter.

"Oh, for heaven's sake, I never thought he did! I just don't know what to talk about. Will he in fact talk to me? George says he's arrogant and rude, and even you implied he was difficult."

"He'll talk to you," Jane said with a chuckle, slicing homemade bread competently against the bib of her apron with a wicked-looking knife. "Talk the hind leg off a donkey when he wants to. Didn't say he was difficult; he's impossible. In some moods. But he's only rude when someone's stupid; you should get along."

"Thank you—I think. But I want to know a little more about him. He's Welsh, you say. Well, of course he is, with a name like Evans."

"Half Welsh. Mother was English. That's where the Nigel came from. Born in Wales, didn't live there long. Father died, mother moved back to Birmingham. Boy picked up odd jobs, whatever he could do. In and out of school, I gather. Mother made money any way she could, but there was never much. When he was twelve or thirteen she died."

How like Jane to skate past the ways Mrs. Evans might have made money. Jane took people as she found them.

"Then it was orphanages and foster homes, and somewhere along the way they found out he could sing. He's bright, as well," she went on, turning sausages. "Got the scholarship to King's—ouch!" A sausage had burst and spat hot fat at her. "You know the rest. Had to leave King's, at a loose end. Hitching here and there looking for work, found it at the cathedral, and got into university. Was going to join the cathedral choir as soon as there was an opening."

Was going to. What chance of that was there now?

"He's lucky he had you to come to when all this broke," I said warmly. Jane shrugged.

"Would have done all right on his own. Not used to people looking after him."

The casual words got under my guard, giving me a sudden sharp picture of what Nigel's life must have been like. My heart twisted. I saw a struggle for survival in a world that didn't much care, a brilliant, good-looking boy who loved music thrown into the twilight world of petty crime and drugs and sleeping on the streets. I shuddered. He'd had to live by his wits, which were considerable. Was it entirely impossible that he had killed in a moment of rage and despair? Things had seemed to be working out, and then suddenly every man's hand was once more against him. That Welsh temper . . . and on the streets of Birmingham, he might well have learned to put a light value on human life.

No. No, it *was* impossible. Please, God, let it be impossible. . . .

"Jane, what did he quarrel about, with the canon? Do you know?"

"Hasn't said anything; I haven't asked. Never does to ask. He'll tell me, in time. They always do."

Well, yes, with Jane they always would.

"Had an idea it had to do with Inga," she began, then broke off at the sound of the back door opening and boots being scraped clean.

In a way Nigel looked better than when I'd seen him in the cathedral. The jeans and summer shirt had been exchanged for decent gray slacks and a good warm yellow sweater—at Jane's expense, I was willing to bet. The boy's hair was neatly combed, and he didn't look quite so pinched and thin. But the fire in his eye that had made him so noticeable was dimmed. Without the armor of his anger and intensity, the naked vulnerability showed.

When Jane introduced us he muttered something inaudible and thumped his package on the table. She and I both ignored his response, or lack of it. Jane filled three plates and handed him one. "Dorothy, can you get the knives and forks? You know where they are."

A proper English breakfast is a thing of beauty and a joy, but not forever. I had no intention of letting Nigel's uneasiness, or mine on his behalf, keep me from enjoying my food while it was hot. Nor, blast it all, to deflect me from the reason—all right, the *other* reason—I had come. I demolished an egg and two sausages before saying casually, "Nigel, I ran into someone you may know, yesterday in London."

My pawn was not so much ignored as shoved off the board. "I don't know anyone in London."

He had no particular accent, Welsh or otherwise. His voice was pleasantly pitched, but sharply dismissive, if not downright rude. He applied himself with concentration to his plate, expertly knifing a bit of sausage onto a forkful of egg and adding a triangle of fried bread to hold the edifice together.

I persisted. "I think you may know him, though. Charles Lambert. He's American, studying right now at the BM, but he was down in Sherebury a few months ago working at the cathedral library."

Nigel put his knife and fork down and, for the first time, looked at me. "Oh. Him. How do you know him?"

"He teaches at Randolph University in America, where my late husband headed the biology department." Something in Nigel's scrutiny made me add, "I met him years ago when I was doing some research for my M.A., a paper on Chaucer. The period is a bit late for him, but he helped with some manuscript questions." I blandly finished my toast while he absorbed that.

The young are often bad at hiding their thoughts, especially when their defenses are down, and Nigel's expressive countenance in particular was not made for concealment. I watched, amused, while he processed the information and altered his opinion of me from Old Busybody Next Door to Educated Woman Who Might Be Interesting.

"So you see," I added mildly, "you do know someone in London."

He had the grace to blush. "Sorry. Talk in haste and repent at leisure. My worst sin. It's the Welsh side coming out." He gave a little sideways grin and flashed those incredible eyes at me in what looked like a practiced technique.

"Indeed," I said austerely. I hoped I hadn't let him see how effective his methods were, even with a woman my age. "Dr. Lambert said something rather interesting about your late employer."

This time the flash might have been unintentional.

I related the conversation. "I did wonder, Nigel, if you had any idea what Mr. Billings was working on. His most recent project."

"No. He kept himself to himself, you know. How well did you know him, Mrs. Martin?"

"Not at all, really, only to say hello to."

"Well, he—they must have told you we'd had a bloody great row the day he died. The curious thing is—I don't suppose you'll believe me—but we usually got on well enough. He was an arrogant bastard—" the blue eyes checked out my reaction to that "—but so long as I did exactly as I was told there was no trouble. I didn't like him, but I did respect him; he was good. And you don't have to believe that, either."

"Is it true?"

"Yes!" The fire was back.

"Then I believe you. 'Good' being, I presume, a description of academic worth, not moral. But if you got along with him, what was the fight about?"

If I had hoped to slip that one in I was disappointed. He couldn't control the white knuckles or the blazing eyes, but he had no intention of answering the question.

"Nothing to do with his work. I never argued with him about that. He'd talk to me about it at times, lecture me, really. I listened; it was worth listening to. But when he got back from Greece in November he was different, closemouthed. I asked him once if he'd got anything worthwhile and he ignored the question completely, said I was to go shelve some books, just as if I hadn't said a word. Made me wonder."

"Did you see anything he was doing? Over his shoulder, as it were?"

He could have been angry at that, but he just shrugged. "Not that interested. I had my own work to do."

So the sore point had to do with something else. Perhaps Jane was right and Inga was involved somehow, though I couldn't imagine how. "Well, that's a pity. Not that it probably matters, but I wish I knew; it nags at me. You haven't heard any gossip, have you, Jane?"

"Not a word."

If Jane didn't know, no one knew, so I might as well give it up. For the moment. I finished my breakfast, trying to make up my mind that Nigel Evans's temper was not sharp enough for murder. I didn't succeed.

I WALKED INTO the cathedral that afternoon just as the bells stopped tolling. The crowd, unusually large, filled the choir; everyone in Sherebury who was idle on a Tuesday afternoon seemed to be there, along with the entire cathedral clergy and staff. Chairs had been set up in the space between the choir stalls and the chancel, and I found one in the back row, settling down unhappily just as the clergy entered and I had to stand up again.

A memorial service is unusual in the Church of

England. Generally a funeral, with or without the Eucharist, serves as the last rite of passage. In this case the dean presumably didn't want to delay some form of healing rite until the authorities finally released the body for burial. Reluctant as I was to take part, I thought he was right. The sooner we could exorcise the fears and ill will generated by this death, the better.

The service was modified from the one for the Burial of the Dead, and like the rest of the *Book of Common Prayer*, it was beautiful and dignified. In the prayers and Bible readings the dean had chosen there was no deliberate attempt to play on the emotions of the mourners. Which was probably just as well, I reflected, because I wasn't certain there were any decently appropriate emotions floating around. I wondered just what other people in the room did feel. Mostly relief, I suspected.

Would anyone here miss the man? The dean, they said, had been unable to locate any family at all. I couldn't pretend the cathedral staff would mourn him; his untimely departure already seemed to be improving morale. The dean was genuinely horrified about the manner of his death, certainly, but I couldn't escape the chilling truth that little sorrow accompanied this death, while someone in the room might well be rejoicing at this moment that his enemy was gone, and he still unsuspected. "But he is in his grave, and oh, the difference to me." I shuddered. Not quite the sort of difference Wordsworth had in mind.

My eyes went involuntarily to Wallingford, still pompously taking Mr. Swansworthy's place; the principal emotion he displayed seemed to be conceit at his temporary elevation in status. I couldn't see Mr. Sayers up in the organ loft; neither could I forget his catty remark about how much he planned to enjoy playing this service.

I spent most of the service determinedly looking at my lap, trying to think about the weather. There was no eulogy, for which I was profoundly grateful; the service leaflet contained a brief biography and a few words of gratitude for the canon's hard work at the cathedral, apparently as much as the dean considered he could say in sincerity. Only a few of the psalms seeped through my barrier of deliberate inattention. *"Thou knowest, Lord, the secrets of our hearts* . . . if the murderer was present, that would give him something to think about, all right . . . *That we should be saved from our enemies, and from the hand of all that hate us* . . . that hadn't happened for the canon, had it? Or perhaps, in a way, it had . . . he was safe from his enemies now, at any rate . . . and then it was over, thank God, and I walked quickly out of the choir, seeking the best way to escape. I did *not* feel like talking.

"Dorothy. Nice to see you again."

I looked up angrily, ready to snarl, and saw the pleasant smile die on Alan Nesbitt's face.

"Sorry—bad timing?"

His voice lost its brightness, and I felt even worse than before.

"No, *I'm* sorry. It's just that I hate this sort of thing—funerals, or memorials, or . . ."

"I don't care for them much, either. I keep thinking about my wife's funeral, years ago now."

That stripped my defenses bare. "For that long?" I stopped walking and turned to him. "I had hoped . . ." My voice tried to wobble; I bit my lip.

"Oh, it's much better than it used to be. Not a sharp pain, just the dull reminder. I'm not sure I'd want to lose that, actually."

"What did your wife die of?" It seemed odd to be talking to him this way, but his calm understanding was like gentle sunlight on this gloomy day.

"Cancer. She was fifty-two. She never saw our first grandchild."

His voice was steady and matter-of-fact.

"We didn't have any children," I said. "I think that makes it worse."

"I suspect that it does. My family has been a great comfort to me. Dorothy, may I buy you a cup of tea?"

I had thought I wanted to be alone, but I couldn't let the sunlight go. Besides, I might be able to find out what the police were doing about the murder. "Bless you. A cup of tea is just what I've been wanting."

Although the institution of afternoon tea is suffering in an England that grows more American every day, cathedral towns maintain the tradition better than most places. Alan chose the nearest of the available shops, Alderney's. The Cathedral Close at Sherebury, like that of Exeter, is lined not only with housing for the clergy and cathedral offices, but, oddly enough, with a few businesses: a pub/hotel (the Rose and Crown), an extremely expensive jeweler, a bank, a small gift shop, and at the far end, near the west gate, Alderney's, in a delightfully rickety Tudor structure with a second story that hangs over the first, exquisite diamond-paned windows, and Tudor roses all over the carved plaster ceiling upstairs in the big tea room.

It was early for tea, but we weren't the only ones with the same idea; the place was crowded. Thinking about death is a thirsty business. We squeezed into chairs at a tiny table in a corner.

"Just tea for me," I said, mindful of how amply I filled the Windsor chair. "Tell me, how are you coming with the investigation?" I had lowered my voice, but the babble around us made an effective screen.

"Slowly," Alan sighed. "There's plenty of evidence, but evidence has to be matched with something. Even in Sherlock Holmes's day, the Trichinopoly cigar ash helped only if one of the suspects smoked Trichinopoly cigars. Do you happen, by the way, to know what they are? I've never heard of them."

"Stop in at 221B Baker Street, and you will undoubtedly be able to consult a monograph on the subject," I suggested. "So you're not able to do any matching?"

"I didn't quite say that, did I? The trouble is, there were far too many people in the church that night. I can hardly give orders for every single soul in Sherebury to be fingerprinted and drop off a sample of hair or clothing or—oh, tea and biscuits, please."

"Earl Grey or Darjeeling?" asked the bored waitress.

"Darjeeling for me," I said.

"For me, too. Are you sure you don't want anything else, Dorothy?"

"Sure. I don't suppose," I said when the waitress had left, "you can tell me why you arrested Nigel? Or let him go again?"

"You know why we arrested him," he said a trifle impatiently. "Motive is our best lead at this point, and his motive is obvious. We had to talk to him. As he wasn't very cooperative we had to bring him in. There wasn't enough evidence to charge him, so we sent him home with a flea in his ear. We're keeping an eye on him."

I sat silent, wondering if I should tell him what I had learned about the verger and the choirmaster. Would it help Nigel? Was I betraying any confidences? Perhaps not if everyone knew about them already.

The waitress came back and plunked down the tea and a plate of assorted biscuits. I absently picked up a chocolate one and started to nibble on it.

"Then you couldn't match up his fingerprints, et cetera, to whatever you have?"

"I can't tell you that, you know."

"No, of course not. Sorry." I finished the chocolate biscuit, picked up a petit beurre, and made up my mind. "You do know about the other good motives? Mr. Wallingford and Mr. Sayers?"

"Dorothy." He lifted his hands, let them drop, took a

deep breath and let it go. "I would much prefer not to discuss, in a public place, the details of a murder case under investigation." The necessity for keeping his voice down made the words come out in a hiss. "Generalities, perhaps—to you—and even that is stretching a point, because I trust your discretion. Now can we change the subject, please?"

Well, I deserved that, I supposed, but it annoyed me all the same. What did he expect me to talk about, the weather and everyone's health, à la Eliza Doolittle? "The rain in Spain," I said with a bright smile and precise attention to the vowels, "stays mainly in the plain. In Hertford, Hereford, and Hampshire, hurricanes hardly ever happen."

He looked at me blankly for a moment, and then crashed his fist down on the table, threw his head back, and roared with laughter. The people at the next table decided it was time to leave.

"By God, Dorothy," he said when he could speak, "you do me good. Stop fiddling with those silly biscuits and have something proper to eat. Waitress!"

ᴄᴏ10ᴏ

"WHICH WAS ALL very well, I thought half an hour later as I headed for home. I'd been jollied into a better mood, but I hadn't got any forrarder, as Agatha Christie used to put it. And why *had* Alan invited me to tea if he hadn't wanted to talk about the murder? Maybe he wanted to ask all the questions. Only he hadn't asked any, had he? Maybe he simply wanted to cheer me up. Maybe he was just a nice man.

The fact remained that I knew no more than I had in the morning and curiosity was killing me. What evidence did the police have that they couldn't "match up" with anyone? Why had they released Nigel? Did he have a really good alibi for the time—good grief, come to think of it, what time period were we talking about? When did they think Billings died? And what nefarious deeds had the man been up to, that he wouldn't tell anybody what he was working on?

Oh, I had plenty of questions, including all of those "whereabouts" queries from that silly list I'd made on the train. But nobody seemed willing, or able, to answer them.

"Aha!" I snapped my fingers, not realizing I had spoken aloud until I saw the glare on the face of the elderly passing clergyman. In his day—a very long time ago, that was—women did not go about getting sudden ideas in the Cathedral Close. It wasn't done. He sniffed and turned his back.

To get from Alderney's to my house, one must either go all the way round the far south side of the Close or cut through the cathedral to the cloister door and across the cemetery. The fog still being thick and disagreeable, I chose the shorter way, which took me right past the Rose and Crown, the best pub in Sherebury. A higgledy-piggledy pile of brick and stone and half-timbering, the Rose and Crown was the pride and joy of the Endicotts. Inga was at this moment probably serving at the bar or doing something about dinner in the kitchen. Why hadn't I thought to ask Inga?

I turned in.

After the cathedral, the Rose and Crown is my favorite place in town, and the Endicotts some of my favorite people. We met years ago, the first time Frank and I came to Sherebury on vacation. Frank hadn't yet learned to drive on the wrong side of the road, so we arrived by train, late and exhausted. Naturally it was raining, with not a bus or a taxi in sight. By the time we'd bought a town map and walked to the Rose and Crown (highly recommended by the sympathetic woman at the newsstand), we were soaked, our luggage seemed to weigh a thousand pounds, and I at least was close to tears from cold and hunger and fatigue.

And the inn was full.

"I can't understand it," the stunning blond woman at the desk kept saying apologetically. "We're *never* booked up except at holidays. There must be something on at the university, or the cathedral. We can put you up starting tomorrow, but not tonight. You say you *walked* from the railway station? But that's a *frightfully* long way!"

She was literally wringing her hands in distress when a large, scrubbed-looking, pink-cheeked man walked in, looked us over, and said to her, "Why don't you ring up the George, darling?"

In five minutes she had called an inferior but more expensive hostelry and obtained a room at the Rose and Crown's rate by mendaciously claiming a reservation gone astray. The pink-cheeked man had whisked us there in his car. "No bother, no bother at all, delighted."

The charming man and wife were, of course, Peter and Greta Endicott. She, we found out, was German; he was as English as the wonderful food he served in the pub. They had an engaging, grave-faced little girl of about three, Inga, who looked likely to turn out as beautiful as her mother. The first time we saw her she was sitting splay-legged in front of the parlor fire, cradling a minute gray kitten in her arms like a baby and crooning to it. She staggered to her feet, came over to me, put the kitten against her cheek, and then held it out to me, saying, "Soft. Feel the kitty?" I was her slave for life.

That kitten was the first of a long line of prize British Blues at the Rose and Crown. Max, the present incumbent, was a lazy rake who spent his days on the mantel of the huge bar fireplace and his nights prowling the neighborhood siring yet more descendants. My Emmy was one of Max's casual offspring; Inga gave her to me with a little speech of welcome when I moved into my house so many years later.

Now, full of my bright idea, I walked in the door. There was no one at the reservations counter in the little hall, only Max, sleepily supervising operations from a cozy nest on a pile of papers as a change from the mantel. He acknowledged my respectful greeting with a wide yawn and stretch as I spotted my quarry. Inga, lovely, leggy, blond Inga, was indeed behind the crowded bar, serving with Peter.

"Dorothy!" Peter boomed when he saw me. "Where've you been keeping yourself, then? We've missed you."

I smiled affectionately at him. "Peter, you old smoothie, you say the same thing every time I walk in here."

"Well, you always stay away too long, don't you?" He turned his head toward an altercation at the end of the bar, cocked an amused eyebrow at me, and walked over to the combatants. "Now, then, how about a nice cup of coffee all round before you go out into the cold, eh?" He firmly removed their glasses and stretched his arms out wide, leaning on the counter. "Had about enough of that lot, haven't you? No coffee, then? Sure? Ah. Well, then, see you next time." There had been no hint of anything but genial courtesy in his manner, but Peter seldom needed force to get rid of troublemakers. There was something about his look when he leaned toward them. . . .

"Dorothy, I've something to show you." Inga, free for a moment, dived under the bar. "Look what I made!" She held it out, her face lighting up in a smile that must certainly, I thought, have already broken a number of hearts. Oh, Nigel, take care!

I squeezed up closer, between the balding man in baggy tweeds and the redhead in the almost nonexistent black miniskirt. "Oh, my. But it's beautiful!" It was a pale pink rose, perfectly modeled, its thin, fragile petals folding into points, the color softly shaded. "What's it made of, china?"

"Sugar." She laughed at my expression, quiet silvery laughter as lovely as the rest of her. "Fooled you, didn't I? Right, one G and T and a lager." She dealt briskly with the orders, still watching my reaction with delight.

"But how on earth did you do it? It's absolutely perfect." I turned it admiringly. "Here, you'd better take it back. My hands are damp and I don't want to melt it."

"It's all right, this one is lacquered. I wouldn't, of course, if it were going on a cake. I'm taking a sugar class up at the university, and we learned to make these this morning."

"You mean this is a cake decoration? It's much nicer than the ones we have at home, more real. They're soft."

"Oh, yes, that's just icing sugar. This is pulled sugar, and it's much better; you can get finer detail, but it's tricky to work with, and quite hot!" she said, looking ruefully at her reddened fingers. "Oh, Dad, we're running short of limes, could you—thanks. Yes, sir, large whiskey. Soda or water?"

"I've always wanted to learn how to do those amazing things with spun sugar, birds' nests and baskets and things like that," I said idly when she could talk again.

"Oh, those are quite easy, actually, we learned them in the first lesson." She leaned across the bar eagerly. "I can teach you, if you'd like. I do them here occasionally, when our pastry cook has the day off. Oh, sorry, would you like a beer or something?"

"Not right now, thanks. I just stopped in to see if you're booked up for dinner." This was obviously no time to try to talk to the poor girl; she was run off her feet. And the Rose and Crown is famous for its food.

"Tonight?" She consulted the reservation book behind the bar. "We're quite full, actually, but we could fit you in early—or late."

"Late, I think, I had a substantial tea." Besides, at the end of the evening she might have some time to sit down and talk, if she weren't ready to fall into bed.

"Right. Nine? Nine-thirty?"

"Nine will be just right."

"Super! See you then!"

That child works, I thought as I went through the cathedral, quiet except for the hum of a place where many people are going about their jobs. On her feet all day at the pub, yet somehow finds time to take a continuing ed class to make her an even better cook. No wonder her parents are dubious about Nigel, who's bright enough, and charming when he wants to be, but doesn't have a splendid record for dependability. But give him a chance, I willed. He'll be all right; give him a chance.

I DRESSED UP for my meal. Good food deserves to be honored. Pink wool jersey and pearls rather flattered my gray hair, I thought, so I wore nothing on my head except a filmy silver scarf to keep it dry. Pleased with myself, I put on my best coat, told Emmy to be good, and set off.

Greta was on duty at the front desk when I arrived. "Lovely to see you again, Dorothy. *Don't* you look splendid!" She was simply dressed in a dark suit and a pale, soft silk blouse, her now-silvering hair swept back from high cheekbones, silver-rimmed glasses perched on a perfect nose. At fortysomething she swept every woman in the place out of the competition, except possibly Inga. I laughed.

"I do my best to keep the tone up, but I must say next to you I look like a refugee from a rummage sale."

"Nonsense, you know quite well you look very nice indeed. We'll put you at the front table and show you off."

Inga seated me in the small bow window where I could see everyone, and took my order. I did go rather well with the dining room, I thought complacently. The pink-shaded candles on each table and the paler pink tablecloths went nicely with my dress, and the sprigs of mistletoe, nestled in evergreen branches, matched my pearls. Greta always made sure her Christmas decorations were simple and tasteful and set the right mood; here in the elegant dining room, with its pale green Jacobean paneling and carved ceiling, they were subdued, while across the hall in the bar the red and gold suited the huge open fire, the low, ancient beams, and the jovial spirit.

Trade was brisk in both rooms. From the bar an occasional loud laugh broke through to our more decorous

retreat. In the dining room one or two tables were beginning to empty this late in the evening, but Inga and her
staff were still extremely busy. She found time, though,
for a typically graceful gesture; when she brought me my
soup she paused to nestle her sugar rose in my hair. "I
knew it would look super there. Enjoy your meal!"

I did, of course, even if I was there with ulterior
motives. It was ambrosial. Purée of chestnut soup was followed by a sublime concoction of fish and prawns in a
delicate sauce whose ingredients I couldn't begin to
guess, served with puff pastry that might have floated off
the plate. There was a perfect salad, crusty homemade
rolls, and finally a dessert of rich custard and tangy fruit,
orange and grapefruit and kiwi, surmounted by a dome
of golden sugar filigree.

"I'll bet you made this," I said as Inga served me, her
pride shining through her weariness. "Look, can't you sit
down and have some coffee with me? I'm the last soul in
the place, and you look all in."

"Whew, thanks." She dropped into a chair, kicking her
shoes off. "Do you like it? It wasn't on the menu; I made it
just for you."

"It's beautiful, *and* delicious. I always eat far too much
here, and I don't regret it a bit." I reached over to the serving table, got another coffee cup, and poured her some.
"Inga, you're ready to drop. You need more help in this
place."

"We'd like to hire someone, but there's not quite
enough business to make it pay. If we manage to expand,
we can do it."

"I didn't know you were expanding. What a good idea;
you certainly could use more room."

"Dad's been wanting to build on. You see, if you
turned this little bow window into a good big bay and
added a bit on the east side, there'd be room for at least
six more tables." Her hands and arms described the

changes and placed the tables with wide gestures, and her eyes sparkled despite the fatigue. "But so far we haven't been able to get permission."

"Oh, naturally, I suppose this is a listed building, being so old and all."

She laughed. "Not likely, not with the way it's been pulled about over the years! There are bits of all the best architectural periods in this building, with a few of the worst, and quite a lot of ghastly Victorian reconstruction. No, there's no problem with the planning people; it was the Dean and Chapter."

I pushed back my plate and tilted my head to one side. "Well, I must say, I knew the cathedral ran a lot of things in this town, but what on earth do they have to do with a pub? I thought you owned the place."

She sighed. "We own the business, but the building belongs to the cathedral. Didn't you know? It used to be somebody-or-other's lodgings a million years ago when the monks were still about the place."

"So why wouldn't they let your dad build his additions? You've all got good taste; you wouldn't do anything that would spoil the look of the Close, if that's what they were worried about."

"No reason, really." She shrugged and lifted her eyebrows. "They said something about an ancient right-of-way there to the east, but we weren't going to close it off, only narrow it by about a meter. Sheer bloody-mindedness, that's all it was." She sipped her coffee and wiggled her toes in contentment. "Oh, that's good. Of course, Dad's going to try again. He thinks things may be different now."

A tiny alarm bell started ringing somewhere deep in my consciousness. "Uh . . . why should they be different now?"

But Inga's face was smooth and unworried. "Well, you see, we don't know for certain, but Dad got the impression most of the Dean and Chapter were in favor of his application. It really is an improvement to the property, and—well, we're good tenants, respectable and all that, and the dean's been really super to us. We think the one who put the spanner in the works was Canon Billings, and now that he's gone . . . oh, it's horrid, of course, but it does look like being good luck for us, doesn't it? How about a cognac before you go home? On the house."

Anything to keep her talking a little longer. "Only if you'll let me pay, and have one with me. Can your parents join us, do you suppose?"

"Dad's still busy in the bar, but Mum might be nearly ready to collapse. I'll ask her."

Sure enough, Greta was finished for the night with her reservations and accounts and the thousand details that make for a successful hotel business, and more than ready for a friendly drink. I felt a spasm of guilt as she sat down and Inga brought in three snifters with a bottle whose label promised liquid gold. These people were my friends. What did I think I was doing, asking awkward questions and taking advantage of their kindness?

Jane's voice echoed in my mind. "Everyone'll think Nigel did it. Convenient . . . no waves . . ." I sighed, mentally, and pursued my questions as gingerly as though I were walking along the edge of a precipice I couldn't see. . . .

"Greta, I understand Canon Billings's death may make your life a little easier."

"What a way to put it!" she said, with her tiny silvery laugh, so like Inga's. "It's true enough, though. And we're not the only ones, I was thinking only today. Now the canon has gone to his reward, Mr. Pettifer will probably get to build his houses, and make a mint of money."

"What houses? Why is it I never know anything about what's going on in this town?"

"Oh, this all happened in the spring before you arrived, Dorothy. You do know him, don't you? Archibald Pettifer?"

"I know of him. Only that he's on the Borough Council, really. Is there any more coffee?"

There was. Inga poured it for us, and Greta went on.

"Mr. Pettifer is a builder by trade, you see. He's been agitating the council to pull down those frightful Victorian slums up near the university and build some council houses. There are so many married students at the university now, and they can't afford anything elaborate, but they need proper housing, and those places don't even have indoor plumbing. Can you imagine, in this day and age!"

"They're run-down, I know," I said a bit wistfully, "but they look solid, and they could really be made very attractive with a little modernization. Wouldn't that be cheaper than tearing them down and starting over?"

"That," said Inga, "is exactly what Billings said."

"Billings again! All right, what did he have to do with *this* one?"

"He sits on the council, too," Greta explained. "And he's always against change—was, I mean. I think, myself, that's why he opposed our application. Not that it was bad, just that it meant change."

"But the two cases are entirely different!" I said warmly. "Yours doesn't destroy anything, but the other—goodness, I do hate to find myself agreeing with Billings about anything, but . . ."

"He also said," related Inga with relish, "that Mr. Pettifer wasn't as interested in clearing slums or providing decent housing as in making a huge profit for himself by putting up cheap, ugly buildings that would fall down in a decade or two. We went to the council meeting that night, and the two of them nearly came to blows."

"So was he the only one opposed?"

"The only one who really cared, but he's—he was—so high-handed he forced a nay vote. Of course Pettifer won't let it alone, and now he'll talk the rest of them round, I should imagine."

So there's someone *else* with good reason to be glad he's dead. I hoped very much I hadn't spoken the thought aloud, but Greta suddenly had a peculiar look on her face. It was time to change the subject.

Inga came up with the new one, after a moment or two of awkward silence. "By the way, Dorothy," she said, fiddling with the clasp on her watch, "have you seen Nigel lately? Since he's staying next door, I mean?" She didn't look at her mother.

"Why, yes, I saw him this morning." Was it really only this morning? "I met him for the first time, in fact."

"How was he?" Inga was still toying with her watch.

"All right, I think. It's hard to tell, when you don't know what a person is usually like. Perhaps a trifle subdued. I *wish* to goodness he'd tell someone what that famous quarrel with Billings was all about! At least, maybe he's told the police, but he won't tell me. Or Jane."

Greta sighed and looked at Inga, a tiny frown between her eyes.

"Oh, I can tell you that." Inga finally looked up at me; she sounded irritated. "It was about me. Or us, really. Mum and Dad and me, I mean—what we've just been talking about. I'd told him that afternoon about the denial of reconstruction permission—we'd just heard— and he got furious. That frightful temper of his came up, and he wanted to have it out with Billings right then. I told him not to be an ass, that it wouldn't do any good, but he wouldn't listen, he never listens, he just stormed off. He came back later to say I was right, he hadn't got anywhere. I can't imagine why he's gone mysterious about it."

Another silence fell. Greta looked at me, her eyes widening, and Inga, looking from her mother to me, drew in her breath sharply. "No. Oh, no. No, you're wrong, you're both wrong. He couldn't have . . . you don't know him, he . . ."

"Inga. I'm on his side. He must have some other reason for keeping it to himself. He's very stubborn, I know that much about him." I tried to defuse the situation. "Maybe he just doesn't want to admit failure."

There was bright color in Inga's pale cheeks, and she started to speak, but Greta put a hand over hers with a warning pressure.

"Perhaps," she agreed, and a trace of long-forgotten German accent crept into her speech. "Or perhaps he thinks he is protecting someone else. He is a fool, but I think perhaps a gallant fool." She reached over and smoothed her daughter's hair back from her cheek in a motherly gesture of love and sympathy that brought a lump to my throat. "Darling, tomorrow we had better call the police and tell them exactly what all three of us were doing on Christmas Eve."

I cleared my throat, pushed back my chair, and stood up.

"I think it's time I went home. I—I'm sorry I brought all this up and caused . . ." Frustrated and embarrassed, I pushed my fingers through my hair and, as I did so, dislodged Inga's sugar rose.

It fell to the polished wood floor and shattered.

✥11✥

I OVERSLEPT WEDNESDAY morning, waking at last with a head full of marbles that rolled around dizzyingly and every now and then crashed into one another with a dull thud. My bed was a welter of sheets and blankets from hours of thrashing about; my pillow was damp with sweat. It's a common enough dream: You're trying to run away from some unknown but horrible thing, but your legs are too heavy and draggy to move. I got up to feed my demanding companion, feeling like crawling into a hole.

Once she was fed I took three aspirin, made some strong coffee, and sat down at the kitchen table to have a talk with myself. If I was having nightmares about running away from something, it was time I faced up to my situation.

Which was, I realized as I stared into my coffee cup, that I had to fish or cut bait. To put it baldly, I had to decide whether to get into a murder investigation with both feet, or to get out of it entirely and leave it to the police. This business of asking leading questions and making everyone extremely uncomfortable had to stop, unless I was prepared to admit that I was vitally interested and intended to pursue, vigorously, an unknown criminal.

I reached for a pad and pen and began slowly to make another set of lists, considering each point with great care.

Why Should I Get Involved?

I'm involved already. I found him; he'll lie there in my memory forever, terrifying me.

No argument there.

Some of my friends, and friends of friends, are suspects. I'd like to do what I can to help them.

Shaky. What makes you think the police can't find the real criminal without your help?

I need something to do.

Oh, come on, now! Why not join a rock band, while you're at it? Act your age!

In response to that mental jeering, I defiantly wrote:

I have many of the qualifications needed by a detective. Years of teaching school have taught me when someone is lying. I'm a good observer, especially here in a foreign setting where so much is unfamiliar. Finally, I'm invisible. Except for a few people who really know me, I'm a foreigner who doesn't count. If I play my cards right, people will talk to me the way they do to strangers on board ship. They'll never see me again, and I know no one who knows them, so it doesn't matter what they say.

I considered that dubiously for a while and then began the second list.

Why Shouldn't I Get Involved?

It's dangerous.

Goodness knows the chief constable's tried to make that clear. But do I believe him? Do I care?

It's unnecessary; the police . . .

Beside the point. Let the police do their thing. Why shouldn't we both be pursuing the truth in our own way? Besides, it's six days now since the murder and they haven't done anything but arrest Nigel and let him go again.

I could hurt people. The Endicotts . . .

That one hit home. I sat biting my pen, considering. I could not only hurt people, I could lose friends, and I needed all I could get in Sherebury.

And yet, was silence about a trouble the way to keep a friend? Should we all pretend nothing had happened, and go about being polite? Wouldn't that, in the end, kill friendship in a more terrible way, by trivializing it?

I took a sip of coffee and put the cup down again. It was stone cold, but no matter. I realized I'd answered my basic question. Whether the chief constable liked it or not—and he wouldn't—I was in this thing. For better, as the marriage service says, or for worse.

Very well, then, how should I attack the problem?

Another list.

Under the heading "Suspects," I set down five names: Mr. Wallingford, the verger; Mr. what's-his-name— Pettifer, that was it—the councilman; Mr. Sayers, the choirmaster; Peter Endicott; Nigel Evans.

That gave me five people I knew, out of all the people in Sherebury who hated him, who had definite reasons for resenting the canon. I studied the piece of paper for a few miserable moments and then decisively struck out the last two names. Motive be damned. I'd known and respected Peter for years, and I was not going to make myself wretched by considering the possibility that he might have murdered anyone. Ridiculous! He was not a violent man. Look at that performance in the bar yesterday. All he'd had to do was look at those two rowdies and they melted away.

Billings wouldn't have melted, said the mean-spirited inner voice.

Shut up. Don't be silly.

He's a big man, Peter. He could easily have . . .

Nonsense!

Peter worked extremely hard to build up his business, and it looks as though he's a little short of money or he wouldn't have his wife and daughter running their legs off. He wouldn't take kindly to . . .

SHUT UP! He stays off the list, and that's that! As for Nigel, he stays off, too, no matter how bad things look. I won't let him be a murderer. He's so young, and so . . . and anyway he'd never work off his temper in quite that way. Shouting, a punch or two maybe—not deliberate murder.

Actually it could have been an accident. From the way Billings's head looked, he could have been shoved against something, or something could have been thrown . . .

I put on a tape of the King's College choir singing some intricate Bach motets. I'd have trouble thinking at all over that; a two-way conversation inside my head would be impossible.

The accident idea had its points, though. Anybody could have gotten into a fight with the man. Jane was obviously right (of course); he had enemies all over Sherebury. I wondered if the police knew who any more of them were. I wondered if they had thought of the accident possibility. I looked at the phone.

And shook my head. No, Alan had told me off pretty decisively yesterday. I didn't intend to pester him with any more questions. Nor was I (here my chin lifted an inch or two) going to volunteer any bright ideas. If he wanted to be official, fine; I'd keep my discoveries to myself and he could do the same, and we'd see who got there first.

At that point my headache began to subside and common sense reasserted itself. *Don't be an idiot, old girl.* This time the inner voice was friendly; Bach had at least achieved that much. *Alan Nesbitt is an intelligent, conscientious police officer who's trying to do his job. And, incidentally, he's a very pleasant man who has been kind to you. So don't go around cutting off your nose to spite your face. You tell him anything he ought to know, and stop pretending to be Nancy Drew.*

Did I in fact know anything he didn't? Probably not. There were a number of things I still wanted to find out, though, several of them concentrated at the cathedral.

I had reached that point in my muddled thinking when Emmy went to the back door and crossly mewed to be let out. I opened the door. The weather was even worse than yesterday, rain and a sort of sleet that managed to be both extremely wet and solid at the same time. Emmy put out one paw, shook it, swore briefly in eloquent Cat, and stalked back into the kitchen.

I shivered, standing beside the door indecisively. I was not eager to walk even as far as the cathedral in that weather. Wouldn't it be more sensible to stay home and tend to domestic affairs until the weather improved?

No, it wouldn't, the inner voice retorted. *It isn't a big house, and you cleaned it properly for Christmas. You're copping out. If you don't want to go a whole hundred yards to the cathedral, go next door and talk to Jane. She's always good for some information, and probably some good advice as well. You could use some of that, old girl.*

Before I could talk myself out of it, I put on a slicker and rain hat and ran next door.

My luck was out. Jane wasn't home. Nigel was.

"She'll be back soon, I think. She's just taken some soup to old—to Mr. Swansworthy. He's down with a bad tummy again. Um—would you like a cup of tea or something?"

"I'd be delighted, thank you," I lied. My acceptance was as reluctant as his invitation, but I'd been given the chance to talk to him. I had to take it.

It seemed, however, that I had misinterpreted his hesitation. He was eager to talk, just uncertain how to introduce the subject.

"You've been talking to Inga," he said as he set a steaming cup of tea before me at the kitchen table.

"My goodness, you do get an early start on the day, don't you?" I said lightly to cover my tightened nerves.

"She rang up," he said. The pause that ensued was what used to be called "pregnant."

"You think I killed him, don't you?"

I didn't spill my tea—quite. "Of course not!" I began, but the intense blue eyes forced me to be honest.

"I don't know," I said. "You had good reasons to hate him. I *hope* you didn't kill the man, and I don't think your temper works that way, but I can't honestly say I'm sure either way. If Inga—"

"Inga didn't do it!" he exploded, standing up with an angry scrape of his chair that jarred the teacups.

"Nigel, sit down!" All the schoolteacher in me came to the top. "We won't get anywhere if you can't discuss this like a reasonable adult!"

He sat. With all the relaxed languor of a panther ready to spring, true, but he sat.

"That's better. Now, what makes you think Inga had anything to do with the canon's murder?"

He would have liked to murder me just then; the eyes flashed blue fire. "I *said*—"

"I heard what you said, or rather shouted. I should think Emmy heard it, next door. You wouldn't have said anything of the kind if you hadn't thought it a possibility, you know. Either you're sure she'll be unjustly suspected, because of her family's quarrel with Canon Billings, or you're sure she did it and can't get the horror of it out of your mind. Which?"

He looked at the floor, sullenly, his arms clasped tightly in the attitude I remembered from Christmas Eve.

"Nigel," I said more gently, "I'm involved in this, too. I'm very fond of Inga, and for some utterly incomprehensible reason I'm growing fond of you, too. Won't you help me?"

He wasn't quite ready to surrender. "Why did you bring up her name, just now? You started to say, 'If Inga murdered him,' or something like that."

I had to think for a moment. "Oh. When you nearly upset the table, you mean. What I started to say was, 'If Inga told you I think you're a murderer, she's wrong.' Or something like *that*. I seem to remember that you speak first and think later, right?"

He unclasped his arms and leaned back in his chair with the first hint of a smile. "Right. Sorry. But I thought . . . oh, well. I may as well tell you, I suppose. Rehearsal for talking to Old Bill."

"Old Bill? Who's he?"

He actually laughed. "The fuzz, I think you used to call them. The coppers. The police. I have been very politely asked to come down to headquarters this afternoon to answer a few more questions."

My mouth felt dry; I took a sip of cold tea. "Questions about what?"

"I won't know that till they ask, will I? I suppose more about where I was that night. I wouldn't tell them much, before, but when Inga rang up she said the police were on their way to the Rose and Crown to talk about it, and she was going to have to tell the truth."

The laughter was gone from his face and his voice. My mouth went drier still. "The truth being?"

"That she was there that night. We both were. At Billings's house."

Now that he had made up his mind to tell me, the story came easily enough.

"I went round to talk to him, after the children's service. I thought he might be in a better mood, full of goodwill toward men, you know. Or at any rate I hoped he would. I need that job badly, and Inga had told me what a fool I was to get on the wrong side of him. After I left the Rose and Crown—"

"For the first time, or the second? You were there twice on Christmas Eve, weren't you?"

"The second time. I went back to lick my wounds after

Billings gave me his tongue-lashing, but I got no sympathy, I can tell you. She got me to admit exactly what happened and told me I'd got what I blood—what I deserved, that they'd fight their own battles, thank you. Her parents gave me a bite and a nip of Christmas cheer, in the spirit of the season, but they were all put out with me, and too busy to bother, in any case. So I left."

"When was this?"

"About five, I think. It was before the rain started, I know, because I walked for a while, round the Close and back again, trying to cool off. Then it started to rain, and my jacket got soaked through in about five minutes. I was just outside the south porch, so I went in thinking I could dry out a bit. That was when I decided to talk to him again, do all the groveling necessary to get my job back."

"And you followed him to his house? Was that wise, dogging his footsteps that way when he was already seriously annoyed with you?"

"Aha! *Now* who's leaping to conclusions? I didn't follow him anywhere, because he wasn't there."

"Wasn't where? At the cathedral or at his house?"

"Wasn't anywhere. I couldn't find him in the church, so I went to his house—"

I interrupted again, leaning across the table. "Nigel, I'm sorry, but this could be terribly important! When was this, exactly?"

"I walked into the church at exactly a quarter to six. I don't have a watch, but the clock struck three quarters just as I was going through the door. The children's service had only been over a little while, but the kids were gone. There were people all over the place, though, getting ready for the late service. So it took me a little while to decide Billings wasn't there."

"And you left through which door?"

"The cloister door, of course. It was the nearest to— oh."

I leaned back again and looked at him grimly. "Exactly. Were there any lights on?"

"Not in that transept, because the electricity is off there. But they still had lights in the rest of the church, and there was quite enough light to see. He wasn't there."

"The police will have to know that," I said firmly.

Nigel squirmed. "Ye-es. But. You see—when I got outside it was raining harder than ever, so I was nearly at his front door, across the Close, before I saw . . ."

He ran down, and I finished for him. "You saw Inga."

He nodded. "The thing was, Mrs. Martin, she was coming out of his door!"

WHAT IT BOILED down to, after we had hashed it out thoroughly, was that he had seen Inga just closing Billings's door behind her. He hadn't particularly wanted to talk to her right then, so he'd turned away, but not, apparently, before she'd seen him and ignored him for the same reason. Later, when the murder was discovered, they'd both brooded about a different interpretation of their actions and gotten scared.

Of course, I thought as I squelched home, not waiting for Jane after all, if they were both telling the truth they each half-suspected the other. That proved the innocence of both. Didn't it?

As soon as the sleet let up a little I headed for the cathedral. I had some questions that needed answering. First of all, I wanted to find out where Wallingford and Sayers were during the relevant period—whatever that was. I had worked out, though, that the children's service was over about five-thirty and people had started coming to the late service about ten-thirty. Surely no one would have dared put the body where it was found after that, so I had five hours to think about.

Second, I wanted to verify my two suspects' motives. I

had no idea how I was going to do that; a bridge to cross when necessary. Third, I was going to try to find out something about the murder weapon, and finally, I intended to figure out where he was murdered.

Sure, you and who else, Sherlock, one of the voices jeered as my sodden shoes slapped against the paving stones of the Close. The sleet had stopped, but not the rain. I ignored the voice, however; I had just thought of another intriguing problem: Why was the body moved to where I found it? Of course it was moved *from* the scene of the crime for obvious reasons—but why *to* a cathedral chapel on Christmas Eve? If you're going to go around moving a body, surely it would be just as easy to take it to some place where there would *not* shortly be thousands of people—Billings's house, for instance. Unless he was killed there, of course.

The cathedral seemed deserted this gloomy afternoon, and very quiet. My wet shoes splooshed loudly on the paving stones; I wasn't surprised when a verger materialized and bore down on me.

"May I help you, madam? Oh, Mrs. Martin, how are you? Dear, dear, dear, how wet you are! Come to the office and let me take that coat, and dry your shoes."

It was one of the vergers I knew by sight, but not by name, a fussy little man with a round little bald head and round little rimless spectacles. He bustled me away like someone shooing hens. I thought he cared more about the unseemly noise and mess I was making than my comfort, but his turning up was providential, all the same.

"Mr. Wallingford seems to be busy these days," I commented casually once I was ensconced in the stuffy little den the vergers used for their office. An electric heater put the temperature somewhere up around August, and I wasn't sorry to shed my coat and shoes for Fusspot to look after. "I suppose Mr. Swansworthy must still be ill?" I sat down casually on the chair with the frayed cane back.

"Humph!" snorted Fusspot (I *must* learn his name, I thought). "There are *some* who come to work whether they're ill or not. And then there are some who make a great show of working, but we'd all be better off without them, if the truth were told."

Oh, my! The little man was obviously bursting with grievances. Pure gold, if I could mine it properly.

"Really?" I said mildly, crossing my fingers and hoping I'd gotten it right. "I thought I saw Mr. Wallingford running about working very hard indeed on Christmas Eve. Around seven, it was." I tried to think of some excuse for my fictitious presence in the cathedral at that hour, but the verger didn't even notice.

"Well, I must say, if you saw him, it's more than anyone else did. We were run off our feet, getting ready for midnight Mass. It's always the same, too much to do and too little time to do it in, and no one to take charge and see it's done properly. And where was our fine Robert when we could have used him? I looked high *and* low for him myself when the others whined they couldn't find him. I want you to know I ended by putting up every one of those candles in the nave myself. Sixteen dozen of them!" He gave a vicious swipe to my left shoe.

I seriously doubted that. Sixteen dozen candles is a good many. However, I didn't want to dry up the flow. "Oh, dear, what a pity. I must have been mistaken, then. I wasn't paying much attention, really, I was actually looking for Mr. Sayers."

He looked at me pityingly as he finished the other shoe. "My dear lady, you really should have your ears checked, as well as your eyes. He was practicing the organ for hours, and I really had to complain to the dean later; it was so loud it gave me a terrible headache. I'm a martyr to migraine, you know, and what with all that extra work, I was nearly prostrated. Here are your shoes.

Would you like to leave your things here while you—er—
do whatever it is you came to do?"

"Oh, no, I couldn't impose." Butter him up, keep him
talking. "You know, I wonder—you do so much here, and
you must hear talk now and again—I'd heard that Mr.
Sayers might be taking another job." Was that a suffi-
ciently diplomatic way to put it?

It wasn't. The little man sniffed. "I hope, madam, that
you do not take me for a gossip. I *never* discuss cathedral
business; I would consider it a breach of trust to do so.
Now I really am quite busy, so if you will excuse me . . ."

I made my apologies and my escape. I'd blown that one,
but I'd learned a good deal first. So Wallingford wasn't
around on Christmas Eve, and Sayers was, eh? It wasn't
proof. The verger could have been someplace out of the
way, and the organ music could just conceivably have been
on tape. But it was an indication, and one I was the more
inclined to accept because I rather liked Jeremy Sayers and
couldn't stand Wallingford. I felt I was doing rather well.

I wandered, idly trying to make out the Latin on some
of the old tombs in the north transept. Did I want to drop
into the library? Would the place where Billings had
worked offer any hints, clues perhaps to his last project? I
went up to the chapter-house door, but it was locked.
That made sense. No librarian, no assistant at least for the
moment. The Dean and Chapter were going to have some
staffing problems to consider when the holidays were
over. I turned from the door and felt as if an icicle were
going down my back.

There he was again, the monk, just gliding past in the
shadows, making no sound, showing no face. I leaned
against the thick, brass-studded chapter-house door,
swallowed, and took several deep breaths. This would
have to stop; I was too old for such shocks. If I was going
to be seeing ghosts all the time, I'd better get used to it
and teach my heart to behave.

All the same, I took a close look around before I left the security of that good solid door. I saw no one, dead or alive, but voices not too far away sounded blessedly normal. Looking down the transept, I saw Mrs. Allenby, with another woman I knew by sight, arranging flowers at the parish altar. I made for them like a frightened child.

"Mrs. Martin, how pleasant," the dean's wife said comfortably. "You know Mrs. Peters, don't you?" The other woman, a soft round little dove with china-blue eyes, lovely white hair, and the complexion of a very soft, faded rose petal, smiled and murmured something gentle.

"Mrs. Martin found our body the other night, you know," Mrs. Allenby went on, and turned to me. "You look as though you're feeling better."

"Much, thank you, although—" I hesitated, and then plunged on, "—although I'd be better still if I didn't keep seeing ghosts. It's unnerving."

Mrs. Allenby cut a red carnation to the proper length while Mrs. Peters deftly snipped off some brownish juniper. "I expect you've seen our monk," Mrs. Peters said softly. "You needn't let him upset you; he's rather an old dear, really."

"I feel sorry for him," said Mrs. Allenby, placidly poking flowers into the brass vase. "He's surely earned his rest after all these years. I asked Kenneth once why he thought the poor man wandered, and he was annoyed; the Church of England doesn't believe in ghosts, officially, you know."

Above our heads the organ suddenly spoke: a series of squeaks and growls interspersed with little runs and chords. "Oh, dear, it's later than I thought, if Jeremy is already choosing the stops for Evensong. We'd best be off, Dulcie. Do you think these look all right, Mrs. Martin?"

"Lovely," I said absently. "I do like to hear Mr. Sayers practice; he's very good, isn't he?"

"Very good, indeed," said Mrs. Allenby approvingly. "I am so glad he's decided to stay."

"You don't mean to say he was planning to leave?" I asked innocently.

"Oh, not seriously, I don't think, but there was some little disagreement with Canon Billings, and for a bit there was talk . . . but now, of course, there's no need for him to think about leaving us. We're extremely lucky to have him; I know Kenneth thinks so, too. Music is so important to the services, don't you agree?"

I agreed, rejoicing in success and trying to figure out how to turn the conversation in the direction of vergers in general and Wallingford in particular when the man himself appeared from the choir. He was moving with the same pompous tread he employed in procession—chin up, leaning just slightly backward—a posture that displayed to great advantage his well-curved front elevation.

"Good h'afternoon, Mrs. Allenby, Mrs. Peters." He bowed, deferentially to the dean's wife, coolly to the flower volunteer. "Mrs. Martin." A slight nod put me firmly in my place. "I shall 'ave to ask you ladies to h'abandon your labors; h'Evensong will begin in . . ." he produced a pocket watch from some hidden recess of his cassock, "h'exactly nineteen minutes."

"Yes, I am aware of the time, Mr. Wallingford," said Mrs. Allenby in as near to a snub as I had ever heard her administer. "Shall we go, Dulcie? Mrs. Martin, I'm delighted to see you looking better." She turned her back and swept away, a performance that both impressed and astonished me, in view of her usual motherly disposition.

The verger had turned ponderously away, ignoring me altogether, but I wasn't about to let him go now that I had him in my web, so to speak. "Oh, Mr. Wallingford," I trilled, "I did want to tell you how beautifully the service went on Christmas Eve." That, at least, was true. "I'm

sure you must have worked terribly hard to get everything so perfectly organized." My fingers were crossed
again.

Wallingford condescended to turn back. The nod this
time was slightly warmer, acknowledging the praise as
only his due. "It is h'always somewhat trying on Christmas
Eve, preparing for the late service whilst tidying up after
the children's service. I may say that I 'ave never, in the
h'eight years I 'ave served this cathedral, been so fortunate
as to partake of h'either tea or dinner on Christmas Eve."

"Why, that's terrible! Do you mean to say you didn't
get a chance to leave at all?" My fingers were crossed so
hard they were beginning to cramp.

"I was, as usual, going about my h'appointed duties
'ere from well before Matins until well past midnight,
with a brief respite for tea and a cold pork pie in the early
h'afternoon," said the martyr to duty. "H'it is gratifying to
know that the sacrifice was h'appreciated. I h'assume,
madam, that you are planning to h'attend h'Evensong?"

"Well, no . . ."

"H'although," said Wallingford weightily, "the rule
states that h'anyone not 'ere in a religious capacity is
required to leave during services, I am prepared to make
an h'exception in your case. I trust that you will not create
any h'undue disturbance should you remain, madam."
Another inclination of the head graciously bestowed his
permission to stay. "Good h'afternoon."

"Good afternoon," I said through gritted teeth. He
moved away toward a small group of tourists, to whom
he spoke officiously. They scuttled out, no doubt with a
fine impression of the warm Christian hospitality the
cathedral had to offer. I felt a twinge in a tooth I suspected was due for a root canal, and unclenched my jaw.
But really, how dare the man! You couldn't have people
wandering about making noise during a service, of
course. But you could be nice about it; you didn't have to

make them feel like worms under your pompous, snobbish feet. What a lazy, self-important, stupid, boring . . ."

"Hello, Dorothy." I whirled, startled.

"Oh, Alan! Alan, did you hear that man? Of all the pretentious, maddening, egotistical . . . and did you know he wasn't here most of Christmas Eve? And he's lying about it? And he's been stealing from the collection, and Billings was just about to get the goods on him, and . . ."

"Yes, I know all those things, and I should be very grateful if you would lower your voice. Sound does carry in here, you know."

"Oh." I lowered it to a hiss. "Sorry, but I was annoyed. *Am* annoyed." I had gotten louder again, and Alan quirked his eyebrows.

"If you're not staying for the service, as I gather you are not, shall we get out of this echo chamber?"

I managed not to say anything until we were safely beyond the cloister door, and then I erupted.

"But if you know, why haven't you done anything about it? It's perfectly obvious—"

"Unfortunately there's a small matter of evidence. No, let me finish. I've been talking to the dean, and I'd best tell you what he said before you begin tilting at several improbable windmills. There is no proof whatever that Mr. Wallingford was responsible for the defalcations. And—" he held up a finger to curb my interruption "—the money has been put back. All of it, they think. Of course they never know exactly how much there should be, but they can compare totals with previous years, and so on. There was a large anonymous gift in this morning's pouch. And as there were only seven people at Matins, all of them known to Canon Richardson, who read the service—"

I couldn't stand it any longer. "But that doesn't make any difference! He can't buy his way out of murder! Just because there's no proof *now* doesn't mean there wouldn't have been, if Billings had gone on digging. And that means—"

"Dammit, Dorothy, I am not Inspector Lestrade or Sugg or Slack or any of the other idiot Scotland Yard detectives your favorite authors love! Don't you think I know all that? The point, if you had let me finish, is that with the return of the money, the dean has decided not to pursue the matter. And without his evidence about the thefts, there is no case whatever against Robert Wallingford."

❧12❧

THE SHEREBURY THURSDAY market was in full cry. At
crowded stalls, ablaze with color in the crystalline light
of a bitter cold, sunny afternoon, vendors hawked their
wares as they had ever since the market was chartered in
1378. Thursday isn't usually quite as important a market
as Saturday, but on this last day of the old year shoppers
thronged the Market Square. The selection was dazzling.
Meats, vegetables, fruits, woolens, tools—those things
had always been sold here. But Brazilian butterflies,
video games, paintings on black velvet always took me
by surprise.

If tacky modern merchandise seemed out of place in
the almost medieval scene, however, the noise of market
day was surely unchanged for centuries. Calls of vendors
in a broad accent I still couldn't understand, the cries of
babies in their prams, the high-pitched gabble of women
bargaining over purchases—it was all very lively and
very English.

I went to the market that day, not so much to buy anything as to soothe my feelings after what had turned into
an awful quarrel with Alan the day before. I had refused
to accept the idea that Wallingford couldn't be arrested
right then, and Alan kept explaining the rules of police

procedure with more and more elaborate patience until I could have screamed, and finally did, right there in the Cathedral Close. Well, yelped with frustration, at least. At that point he became coldly reasonable and suggested that I needed some tea, and I became coldly polite and replied that what I needed more was some intelligent advice, and after *that*, of course, there was nothing to do but march off home, where I burst into tears of pure anger.

I was still angry, none the less because I knew he was right. Logic was on his side. But logic be damned, I still wanted to *do* something. My choice of the market as a distraction was perhaps unfortunate, because I could certainly do something there. I could spend money.

There is something stimulating about crowds of people eagerly bent on commerce. Those who run shopping malls all over America (and, increasingly and disgustingly, England) make fortunes on the principle. I bought in rapid succession several things I didn't need at all, including some rich tea cakes that would be ruinous for my figure.

The only thing I almost needed was a pair of festive earrings to brighten up the old party dress I planned to wear to Jane's New Year's Eve party tonight. It was a black beaded affair, my standby for years. I was really very fond of it, but for New Year's Eve it needed a little glitz. As I doubtfully studied the effect of gold filigree, a face appeared behind me in the mirror.

"Inga, my dear! What do you think of these?"

I hid apprehension behind cheeriness. How was she feeling about me? Would she snub me? Blow up?

"They're all right," she said dully.

I turned from the mirror then, and we looked at each other for a long moment. Her face was as pale as her hair.

"Inga, I—"

"Mrs. Martin—" she said at the same instant.

"You haven't called me Mrs. Martin for years," I said

sadly. "Oh, my dear, don't look at me that way! It'll be all right, really it will." I put my arms around her shoulders and pulled her close, and after a moment she relaxed, with a long, quavery sigh.

"We can't talk here," I said when I was sure she wasn't going to cry. "May I buy you a cup of tea?"

It was a little early yet; the nearest shop had a vacant table or two. We got our tea from the serving line and then settled ourselves and our purchases and unbuttoned our coats.

"That's a smashing hat," said Inga in an admirable attempt at lightness. "It looks like something from a Carole Lombard flick."

I tilted the burgundy soup-plate concoction a little farther over one eyebrow. "It's old enough," I said. "It belonged to my mother. I couldn't bear to throw it out. Wearing it always lifts my spirits, and they needed it today." I gave up the pretense. "Inga, how is Nigel?"

"He's not in jail yet," she said a little shakily. "I reckon that's something to be grateful for, anyway. He was raked over the coals pretty thoroughly yesterday, but they sent him home in the end. Dorothy, I'm scared!"

"So am I, my dear," I said, glad to be 'Dorothy' again. "But we'll just have to keep up our courage. We know Nigel is innocent, and . . . what?" For a hint of a smile had appeared on her face.

"Oh, nothing, really. I just suddenly thought how much he would hate being called 'innocent.'"

I thought of those wicked blue eyes. "Yes, well, I guess it's not quite the word, is it? Really, you know, we should have more confidence in his ability to get himself out of trouble. He's had a lot of practice."

Somehow I'd managed for once to say the right things. We finished our tea in companionable silence. The air was clear again; Inga's color had returned, and along with it her composure.

"So what are you wearing to the party tonight?" I asked when we were back in the marketplace. "You are going, aren't you?"

"Yes, Mum and Dad said they could manage without me for one New Year's Eve. We're booked up, of course, but a set meal is easier to serve. And I've the most smashing new frock—oh, *Lord*, look, there he goes!"

I turned and saw only a small crowd of people gathered round a stocky, red-faced, bull-necked man I didn't recognize. "There who goes?"

"That's Mr. Pettifer, you know, the councillor. I'll bet he's making a speech. Well, it's a safe bet, really, he always is."

"Come on, then, I want to know what's going on." I moved closer, but apparently it was a private speech, because the stocky man gave me an irritated look, turned his head away, and lowered his voice slightly.

". . . need to develop . . . increase traffic by at least forty percent . . . younger buyers . . . sentimental nonsense . . . no more trouble about permission . . ."

The snatches that reached us, along with his gestures at the building in front of the little group, told the story. I turned to Inga in dismay. "Oh, *no!* He's going to turn that gorgeous old building into a shopping mall! What is it, really?"

"The Town Hall, but it's going to be vacant soon. They're putting the city offices in the new Civic Centre out near the university. I don't know why they keep moving everything farther away. This was really convenient for official business, and it's beautiful inside, too, all linenfold paneling and beamed ceilings. And what are they going to do about the Hall? It's been the meeting place for town activities for centuries. It's a *frightful* pity to cut it about into tacky little shops!"

"It hasn't happened yet," I snapped.

"It will," she said with a sigh.

"Who are those people he's talking to?"

"I don't know all of them, but the bald one is on the council, and that woman in the frightful tartan coat owns a chain of gift shops, and I think the man who looks sort of Michael Caineish is John Thorpe, the estate agent. He's gathering all the forces together, you see. I do wish progress didn't always seem to mean pulling something down, or messing it about."

She glanced at her watch. "Oh, heavens, I've got to fly or Mum'll be having seven fits. I'll see you tonight."

"I can't wait to see your dress!" I waved, and she was off. I was glad she was feeling better. But for how long?

I wandered unhappily, letting my feet take me where they would while my mind pursued its own paths, and they took me, as usual when given free rein, to the cathedral. I found myself in the nave with no idea how I had gotten there, but willing enough to pass some time in its vast peace and stillness, tangible as water in a pool. Only a handful of people were in sight; I would be in no one's way if I relaxed for a while.

For a long time I simply sat, bathing in serenity, letting my mind drift. Even on this bright day the nave dozed in the softened light of medieval stained glass. Stirrings of sound somewhere in another part of the cathedral only intensified the fundamental quiet.

How odd, really, if one thought about it, that after all that had happened this place should still be a retreat of tranquility. Or perhaps not so odd. The present crisis must be, to this vast and venerable pile of stone, but a tiny, fleeting stain on the fabric. It had seen far worse down through the centuries. The worst that man could invent could have no lasting impact on the essential character of the cathedral. If we were to burn it down, I thought dreamily, leaving nothing but a lacy Gothic shell, it would remain a refuge and a haven, like Tintern Abbey.

But what of the people? To be selfish, what about me?

The cathedral might survive no matter what, but I still didn't like the stain. I wanted to scrub it out. Until this was settled there was an uneasiness, a disquiet. Until this was settled, I couldn't settle—into a new community, into a new life.

That, I realized, was at the heart of it. That was why I went on meddling in something distinctly unpleasant that was really none of my business. Because this murder had involved me almost from the beginning, I had to stay involved to the end or lose the sense of belonging that I had just begun to establish. No matter how much of a fool I looked to other people, this *was* my business.

The uneasiness had taken up residence between my shoulder blades; I couldn't sit still any longer. I set off in search of the dean. The time had come when I had to talk to him about Messrs. Sayers and Wallingford. And come to think of it, what might he know about one Archibald Pettifer?

The play of light in the nave was like music made visible. In bright chords of color it reflected from wall to wall, swirled and eddied in the dust motes like a chant. One could almost hear it.

I *could* hear it; the chant was real, though no singer was visible. Mystified, I followed my ears and saw the dean, fully vested, and—surely that was the bishop with his crozier!—both of them behind an acolyte who was swinging his censer and making his way down the south choir transept. Moving quietly at a discreet distance, I stepped after the little procession.

They stopped at the last side chapel before the cloister door. In my position, sheltered behind a tomb, I couldn't hear the words of the prayers that the dean and bishop were intoning so softly, but their intent was clear. I didn't need the clouds of incense that were enveloping altar, clergy, and all to tell me that a cleansing was taking place here. This holy place had been desecrated with the intent of murder, if not the actual act. Evil had been here, and could not be allowed to remain. I stole a little nearer and heard the words of the Litany rise with the incense. "From all evil and mischief; from sin; from the crafts and assaults of the devil; from thy wrath, and from everlasting damnation . . ." With the others, I murmured in response, "Good Lord, deliver us."

The service was short. As the little procession turned to go, I blinked the incense out of my eyes, and then blinked again. The light in the Norman transept was never good, but surely there was a fourth figure in the procession? Humbly bringing up the rear, a monk walked with lowered head and silent, sandaled feet. I turned my head away, but not this time in fear. It was only right to give him his privacy, poor man. How many hundreds of years had it been since any kind of service had been held at that altar, his own particular place? He was worshiping in his own way, I supposed, and it was right that he should do so. What matter whether he was alive or dead?

When I looked again he was gone. They were all gone. But I hadn't imagined the whole thing. Clouds of incense still hung in the air. I suppressed a cough and moved away quietly, feeling as if I had intruded on something private, a family affair.

I waited about, reading tomb inscriptions, until the dean emerged from the vestry.

"How nice to see you, Mrs. Martin," he said, smiling. It was nearly his old smile, without the lines of worry that had shadowed it for the past week. Serenity shone once more from his kind face. Perhaps the service had exorcised the demons from the chapel; certainly they were gone from the dean. "I'm glad you were there just now," he went on. "This has surely been as trying for you as for all of us. Perhaps it will be better now."

"It is better, thank you. I didn't mean to intrude on the service, though; that's why I stayed in the background. I

might have known you would see me. Did you see . . . ?"
I bit off the question, but the dean's smile turned almost
to a grin.

"Our friend? Was he there? It wouldn't surprise me.
But I didn't see him. I never see him, if I can help it."

I chuckled. "No, it wouldn't be proper, would it? You
know, the odd thing is, I've seen him twice before, and he
terrified me, both times. This time I just felt rather sorry
for him. Perhaps I'm getting used to seeing ghosts."

His face changed; he looked worried and upset. "You
know, Mrs. Martin, there really are no such things as
ghosts; I shouldn't have joked about it. If we think we see
odd things now and again in an old place like this, they
can be nothing more, really, than shadows of things that
were, with no power to harm us. If you were frightened,
there must be—something else. I'm sure I don't know
what," he ended rather helplessly.

"No, it's all right, I'm just being an idiot, I expect. But I
did want to talk to you about—what happened here. If
this is a bad time I can come back . . ."

"No, no, of course not. I'm entirely at your disposal
until Evensong. Would you like to come across to the
deanery, or will the little study do?"

I said the little study would be fine, and the dean led
the way, securely in charge again. I felt uneasy. He
thought I was troubled by a crisis of conscience or some
such spiritual malady; how would he react to my playing
detective?

"There now," he said when we were both settled in the
squashy old chairs, "what can I do for you?"

I sat in silence for a long moment, considering how
to begin. "I don't know if this is going to make any
sense to you," I said finally. "I'm not sure it makes sense
to me, to tell the truth. But you see, I've been—looking
into Canon Billings's murder."

The dean cocked his head to one side, inquiringly.

"Sort of—talking to people. Trying to find out what happened. Oh, I know what you're going to say," I added as he opened his mouth. "And I agree with you. The police are the people to do this, and they're quite competent, and all that. But somehow I can't leave it at that. It's partly that I love this cathedral," I mumbled, embarrassed at displaying emotion in front of an Englishman, "and partly that I found the body, and partly that I rather fell for Nigel Evans and want to make sure he's well out of it, and—oh, I don't know, really. But I've been asking a lot of questions, and there are some I'd like to ask you, that's all." There, it was out. And it sounded quite as silly as I expected it to.

"I think that's perfectly natural," said the dean. "So long as we agree that I may not be able to answer in some cases, ask me what you like."

I gave him a grateful smile. Someday I may learn not to underestimate people.

"I should have known you'd understand. All right, then, I won't try to be tactful. First of all, there are lots of rumors circulating that both Mr. Sayers and Mr. Wallingford had good reason to dislike the canon, in fact that they both stood to lose their jobs if he had his way, and Mr. Wallingford might face a term in jail. Can you tell me anything about any of that?"

"I've discussed part of this with the police, of course. They don't seem to have got hold of the rumors about Mr. Sayers yet, and I didn't think to tell them. . . ."

"I may have to, you know. I promised myself I wouldn't get cute with anything important. As a matter of fact I doubt I'll find out anything they don't already know; it's just that I might interpret it differently."

"Yes, of course you'd look at things with a fresh eye, as a newcomer. As to Mr. Sayers, it's not much more than a rumor, and I'd be glad to lay it to rest, if I can. It's true that Canon Billings did not approve of some of the choices about the music. He was inclined to be extremely conservative. I have a tin ear, as my dear wife is always telling me, so I did give some consideration to what Canon Billings said. However, enough people had come to me to compliment me on the improvement in the music since we hired Mr. Sayers that I was disposed to be cautious. I discussed the matter, in fact, with members of the music faculty from the university. They universally advised me that Mr. Sayers was the best thing that had happened to cathedral music in years, and that I could count myself extremely lucky to have him. I would not have allowed him to be dismissed under any circumstances."

That sounded final enough. Except, except . . .

"Did he know that?"

"I had mentioned to Canon Billings—"

"No, sorry, but I mean Jeremy Sayers. Did he know his job was safe?"

"I certainly never gave him any other impression," said the dean, looking a little startled. "I assumed he knew nothing about the controversy, and needn't know."

"Oh, he knew, all right." Were even the best clergymen always a little naive? "He was quite certain he was going to be fired any minute." The dean raised his eyebrows. "He told me so himself."

"Oh, dear." Naive, perhaps, but never stupid. He saw the implications clearly enough.

"Right. I don't suppose you know where Sayers was between the children's service and midnight Mass?"

"It is his habit to rehearse for an hour or two between services, but I can't say for certain. I went home for a nap; I'm not getting any younger, and the late service is rather strenuous."

"I see." We looked at each other, and I gave up that unproductive topic for another. "And Mr. Wallingford? I know he's in the clear now, but how much trouble was he really in before?"

The dean didn't question how I knew. "A great deal, I'm afraid. Here, again, the matter is virtually public knowledge. There's really no doubt that he was stealing from the cathedral. The treasurer and I looked into the matter thoroughly when the totals began to come in at about half of what they ought to be, both from the collections and from the restoration fund boxes. It came down to Mr. Wallingford. There was simply no question that the money disappeared whilst under his responsibility, but we couldn't imagine how he did it, and there was no proof. There is still no proof, and no explanation, but as the money has been approximately made up and it seems certain Mr. Wallingford will be more careful in future, we have decided to pursue the matter no further."

"It has been made up, you're sure? I mean it isn't just fudged bookkeeping or something?"

"Oh, no, the money came in yesterday morning, in cash. Mr. Wallingford called attention to it, as a matter of fact, when he brought in the money from Matins. Said something about what a nice Christmas present. We could scarcely believe it, all those lovely new hundred-pound notes."

"You're sure he's the one who put it there."

"As sure as we can reasonably be. It would be most unusual for a real donation of that size to be made anonymously, in cash. Unprecedented, in fact. You do realize we're talking about several thousand pounds."

"Good grief, no, I had no idea it was as much as all that!"

"It's been going on for some time," the dean said dryly. "As you can imagine, we are very glad to have the money back."

"I'm sure you are, but it doesn't alter the fact that Mr. Wallingford had excellent reason to fear Canon Billings."

"No." The dean spread his hands and sighed. "But what can we do? There is no proof of anything."

I saw no reason to tell him that Wallingford was lying about his activities on Christmas Eve. The dean had enough to worry him. But he went on.

"There's no denying, I'm afraid, that Mr. Wallingford has proved unsatisfactory in many respects. He is sometimes quite rude to visitors, and nothing I say seems to help. He can be maddeningly pompous, and never seems to be where he is supposed to be; I've been looking for him all day to arrange some details about tomorrow's services, and he seems to have vanished. But now that he's put back what he's stolen—and I'm quite sure that's what he's done—it would be most unfair to sack him. In fact," he shook his head ruefully, "I fear we're stuck with the man for life."

"And that's because Canon Billings died, too," I said soberly. "There doesn't seem any end to it. Nigel will get to keep his job—at least I suppose he will?"

The dean nodded.

". . . and his place at the university. The Endicotts probably get to build on their addition, and Mr. Sayers goes on producing glorious music here. On the other hand, you have to keep putting up with Mr. Wallingford, and that Mr. Pettifer will go about wreaking destruction in Sherebury unopposed."

"Oh, I do hope you're wrong about that, Mrs. Martin," said the dean with a frown. "That is one matter in which I was very much in agreement with Canon Billings."

"I suppose no one is all black," I agreed. "If only he'd gone about things differently, maybe people wouldn't have hated him so much. Maybe he'd still be alive."

"It was a mistake to bring him here," said the dean, more to himself than me. "He was no good with people; he put their backs up. I must admit there were times when he might have told me eggs were eggs, and I'd have disagreed on principle. However," he sighed, "we mustn't judge him too harshly. He was brought here to do a job, and he did it very well. He was a first-rate scholar, you know."

"Oh, that reminds me. Do you know what he was working on when he died? I ran into someone who seemed to think he was being mysterious about it."

"He was. I asked, when he came back from Corinth, whether the trip had been productive, and if he'd had any difficulty with the earthquake—they had a mild one when he was there, you know—and he was rather vague. He did say one thing, though, I recall. It was in a Chapter meeting. He quite calmly said that we should have to build an addition to the library, because soon there wouldn't be enough space for everyone who wanted to work there. Everyone just stared at the man, because if you've ever seen two readers in our library at once, it's more than anyone else has done. And he said he meant, of course, after his book was published, and then dropped the subject. I remember, because it's the only time I ever heard the poor chap make a joke. He said that St. Paul was going to be so famous at Sherebury that St. Peter would be jealous—referring to the dedication of the cathedral, you see."

"Well, it's not much of a joke, but it's odd, all the same. It does sound, though, as if the new book was to have something to do with St. Paul. I suppose I'll have to ask George Chambers. He works in the same general field; the canon might have talked to him about it."

High overhead, two of the cathedral's great bells began to speak. "Heavens," said the dean, "that's the Evensong warning. I'm sorry, Mrs. Martin, I fear I've been of very little help."

"At this stage, I don't know what will be a help and what won't, but thank you, Dean. It's always good to talk to you; I feel better, anyway."

The two bells rang me home.

❧13❧

I KNOCKED ON Jane's door unheard, opened it, and plunged into a sea of music, color, and laughter.

Nigel materialized at my side with a steaming mug of mulled wine. "There's champagne if you'd rather," he shouted over the party.

"No, this is lovely, thanks. Cheers!" I raised my cup in salute. "You're looking splendid this evening, I must say. Where on earth did you get the outfit?"

He looked down with a kind of mocking pride at his Edwardian dinner clothes, brocade waistcoat, floppy tie, and all. "Oxfam," he said with a grin, naming the charitable organization that runs secondhand shops all over England. "They do cater to the poor and needy, don't they? You're rather grand, yourself."

I'd settled for some modest and ancient diamond studs in my ears, but I was reasonably pleased with my appearance, and touched at Nigel's appreciation. "Thank you, my dear. But I'm dying to see Inga's new dress. Where is she?"

He gestured with his head toward the other side of the room.

I gasped. The "smashing frock" was a little—very little—peach satin number that clung in all the right places and revealed just how marvelous those long, long legs really were. She saw us then, and said something we couldn't hear.

"Excuse me." Nigel was gone, drawn by the magnet.

I drifted to the buffet table. Jane makes no claim to being a gourmet, but she is an excellent plain cook, and she is generous. Cold meats, cheeses, homemade bread, mince pies—I filled my plate and settled down to some serious eating, partly to offset the effects of the alcohol I intended to consume.

When the last crumb was gone I made my way through the crowd to the piano, where Jeremy Sayers sat playing popular music as brilliantly as he played organ classics at the cathedral. He was tolerating the crowd of distinctly amateur singers-along with remarkable charity, for him, relieving his feelings by spinning now and then into a cadenza or two, a key change, or a tricky improvisation that no one even tried to follow.

He looked up at me and segued into a chorus of "Poor Jud is Dead," from *Oklahoma!*, with malicious emphasis. I may have been the only one, in that English crowd, who recognized the song and remembered its words celebrating the advantages of being dead. When he was sure I'd gotten the point, he switched to "Who's Sorry Now?"

I choked on the remains of my wine. Really, the man was wicked! He winked at me; a series of cascading arpeggios led to a decorous version of "Greensleeves." The ragged chorus of singers began again.

I saw Jane, finally. She was off in the corner with the two bigwigs of the evening, the vice chancellor of the university and Dean Allenby. She waved, but there was no way she could get through the crowd to say hello. I scanned the room for a place to sit.

Really, everyone in town was there! Well, nearly everyone. I was pleased not to see Mr. Wallingford, and surprised that George and Alice Chambers didn't seem to be here. But Archibald Pettifer (what was *he* doing here, I wondered) was making his usual speech, holding forth next to the buffet table. The fussy verger didn't appear to be listening; neither did Mrs. Alderney from the tea shop. Dr. Temple was, though; he was storing up more gossip.

And who was that, just coming in the door, his head easily visible over the rest? He came straight across the room to me.

"Dorothy, will you let me tell you how stunning you look, or aren't you speaking to me?"

I think I blushed. "I *am* sorry, Alan. I was being very stupid yesterday. You were right and I . . ."

"No, it was my fault. I was irritated and frustrated myself, and I took it out on you. In short, I behaved like an ass, and I apologize."

"You did not. You were perfectly civilized. I was the one who lost my temper . . ."

I broke off once more; Alan's hand was going to his face in an effort to hide a smile.

"All right, all right!" I grinned and held out my hand. "You were a pompous prig, and I acted like a two-year-old. Truce?"

He took my hand and shook it ceremoniously. "Shall we try to find a place to sit down?" he suggested.

"You can see over the crowd—you lead the way."

Jane's house, like most on the street, spreads up rather than out, something like a New York brownstone. The party occupied most of the first two floors, but we found a tiny, forgotten-looking room off one landing with a couple of shabby armchairs, fortunately empty. We sank into them.

"Alan, you look tired." He sat with long legs stretched out in front of him, his arms limp at his sides. His usually ruddy face looked washed out, and the laugh lines around his eyes seemed to droop.

"It's been rather a frustrating day. My life consists so

largely of meetings, which I detest. Four today, not one of which accomplished anything. Sheer waste of time. I didn't get back to my office until after six, and then I had to tick off one of my chief inspectors; the chap's made a complete botch of investigating a drugs case out in Dilham, and we shall have to start over from the beginning. I do hate meddling with what the men are doing, but in this case I had no choice. Ah, for the days when I was really a policeman, not an administrator." He stretched and yawned massively. "Sorry."

"What you need is a drink. Let me get you one; what would you like?"

"Can't. I let my driver off this evening, so I'm driving myself."

"Can't you have just one? Surely that wouldn't affect a man your size."

"No, but I can't afford the risk. Suppose I were involved in an accident? Even if it were someone else's fault, the slightest hint that I'd been drinking—" He shook his head at the idea. "No, but I could use something to eat, now that you mention it." He started to struggle out of the deep chair, but I motioned him back.

"Nonsense. I napped early this evening while you were struggling with subordinates. I'll be back; save my place."

When I returned with a loaded plate, a fork, a napkin, and two cups of coffee, all piled insecurely on a small tray, Alan's eyes were shut and his head was nestled into the wing of his chair. I stood, irresolute, but a burst of laughter from a group of Jane's kids in the next room woke him.

"Here's some sustenance, but you ought to be home in bed, you know." I set the tray down on the table between us. "Why on earth did you come to this party anyway?"

"For a sensitive and discerning woman," Alan said, forking some roast beef between two slices of crusty bread, "you can be remarkably obtuse." He added mustard and horseradish and took a large bite. "Ahh! That's the first food I've had since breakfast."

"What do you mean, obtuse? I am not!"

"I came to the party"—he popped a pickled onion into his mouth— "to see you."

"Alan, you *don't* mean you have to question me *again*," I wailed. "Not at a party!"

He put his fork on his plate, and his plate on the tray, with deliberation, and wiped his mouth with his napkin. Then he turned in his chair to look straight at me, tenting his fingers in his favorite gesture. "I—came—to—see— you," he said, one word at a time, and turned to pick up his sandwich.

"Oh. Oh!" I had no response. My brain had turned to lemon Jell-O.

"Dorothy." His tone was softer. "It has been a very long time since I've met a woman with wit, intelligence, charm, and enough cheek to snap at me. You're stimulating to talk to, pleasant to look at, and I enjoy your company. Since Helen died I've lived for my work, but that isn't good for me or the job, and I'm close to retirement in any case. I've suddenly realized I'm becoming a bore and, as you said, a prig, and I need to—'lighten up,' I believe the American expression is. So I decided to come to Jane's party to spend some time with you. And I end by making a speech."

He picked up his sandwich.

"Well," I said, and cleared my throat, "as conversation, it beats the rain in Spain. But I do think perhaps you've addressed too many committees today; the content is quite pleasant, but the style is a trifle dry. I for one need a glass of champagne; are you *sure* you won't? Don't forget the boring prig lurking in the background."

"Ouch!" Having finished everything else, he ate a mince pie with great satisfaction, drank some coffee, and heaved himself out of the chair. "Quite right. I'll find someone to take me home. Lead me to the dissipation."

We had some champagne that tasted so good we had some more, and then we went over to join the group at the piano. Alan turned out to have a pleasing baritone and a good memory for the oldies. Many were British and unfamiliar to me, but I added my tentative soprano to the ones I knew. When Nigel decided to join us, his magnificent tenor so outshone the rest of us that we dropped out, one by one, and turned him and Jeremy Sayers loose to do their professional best.

Which was very good indeed. The room quieted to listen, a remarkable compliment considering that most of us had by then achieved that condition the English used to call "nicely, thank you."

"It will be a great pity," I murmured to Alan when they had finished to loud applause, "if that boy doesn't go on to be a singer." I watched him grinning and bowing, looking happier than I had ever seen him.

"There are more secure careers," said Alan as we found a couple of chairs near the fire, "but he has the talent, no doubt about it. Perhaps now that the late unlamented is out of the picture he'll be able to go ahead at university and work at music as well, two strings to his bow."

I turned to him eagerly. "Then you don't really suspect him anymore?"

"I didn't realize you cared quite so much, Dorothy," Alan replied in a very gentle voice. He glanced around, but no one was near enough to hear us above the noise. "Please remember I'm not in charge of the case, but you must realize no one can be left out of consideration yet. Their own admissions put both Nigel and Inga in very compromising positions at the relevant time. Of course, if they're both telling the truth, they're both out of it, especially if each genuinely suspected the other. Inga says she was never actually in the canon's house, that she opened the outer door to knock on the inner one, but no one answered. When Nigel saw her she was just letting the outer door close behind her. Their stories are being checked very carefully." He looked tired again. "We'll not leap to any conclusions, you know."

I felt old. "I do know, Alan, but I'm worried, all the same. Even if you give them a clean bill of health, and I'm sure you will, in the end, Nigel's still not out of the soup, really. George Chambers doesn't like him any more than the canon did, and I think he'll just be waiting for Nigel to get himself into trouble."

"George Chambers doesn't like any young man at the university who attracts that much attention from the young women at the university."

"You mean because he distracts them from their studies, or something?"

"He distracts them," said Alan with great precision, "from George Chambers."

I was stunned. "You can't be suggesting—George? Chasing the coeds? Not *George*!" A vision arose of the White Rabbit loping across campus after a short-skirted woman student.

"There was a bit of a scandal a few years ago, actually. An American girl, over on a Fulbright scholarship. Her parents got wind of it somehow and raised a stink, and she got bundled off home. It was hushed up, of course. I don't believe Alice ever knew. That calmed George down for a bit, but I hear hints every now and then that he's feeling his oats again."

I shook my head incredulously. "I find it really hard to believe that any girl that age would fall for George's tired line. It wasn't just some sort of ghastly misunderstanding?"

Alan chuckled—well, it was more of a snort, to tell the truth. "Dorothy, you're a nice woman. If you don't believe me, ask the vice chancellor. He knows all about it."

At that moment there was a fresh burst of noise accompanying the entrance of more guests, so I had to ask Alan to repeat what he had said.

"He knows the whole story about George!" he trumpeted.

"Were you calling me, sir?"

And there they stood, George and Alice, just arrived and looking extremely annoyed.

When one is confronted at a party by an old friend whose sex life one has just been discussing, in unfavorable terms, an interesting social situation arises. I stood dumb, a bright smile stiffening my face.

"There you are, George. Just talking about your book," said Alan lightly.

"What about it?" George snapped.

My brain began to work again, and I picked up my cue gratefully. "Only that you've never really told us all about it, and we're dying to know." It wasn't a great recovery line, but maybe George would buy it.

"Too noisy in here to talk about anything," he growled, and walked away.

"I'm so sorry," said Alice, looking harassed. "He's in a really filthy mood, I'm afraid. He forgot about the party and came home late from the university, and then was frightfully annoyed at having to dress up and go out again. He'll be more human when he's had one or two, I expect. And then, you see, you asked the wrong question. The final revision of the book for the press doesn't seem to be going well, and he's prickly as a hedgehog on the subject."

"Oh, dear, poor man. I'll be sure to avoid mentioning it, then. Thanks for warning us, Alice," I murmured, and Alan pulled me far enough away to heave our sighs of relief in decent privacy.

"Thanks for the quick thinking, Alan; I couldn't say a word."

"I noticed. You reminded me of a goldfish; your mouth was opening and closing and your eyes were bulging."

"You pay such lovely compliments. No wonder your social life is a bit slow. Do you suppose George caught on?"

"Probably. But it doesn't matter, if Alice didn't. I'm going to ask Jane if there's anyone here who lives out my way and might give me a lift, and then I'm going to have one more glass of champagne. It's nearly midnight, did you realize? We must have something to toast the New Year."

He had not yet returned with our drinks when I became aware of a sound that had, I realized, been underlying the party noises for a few moments—a buzz of alarm growing in the room. What on earth . . . then I heard what the others had already heard. Sirens. Lots of sirens, loudly insistent, and lots of flashing lights reflecting off the windows and walls. With nearly everyone else, I stepped out the front door and peered down to the end of the street.

Fire trucks. It looked like dozens of them. Smoke billowing, and then a tongue of bright fire bursting forth. For one dreadful, heart-stopping moment I thought the cathedral was on fire, and then I saw.

It was in the Close. It was a house. It was—it couldn't be, but it was—Canon Billings's house.

෴14෴

I RELUCTANTLY CRAWLED out of bed a little before noon. Happy New Year, indeed.

Emmy let me sleep because I'd fed her before I went to bed at five or so, when most of the excitement was finally over. I couldn't have slept before that if I'd wanted to, what with all the noise coming from the Close, and my anxiety about the cathedral and the other houses.

Everybody, of course, had flocked out of Jane's house when we heard the commotion. Midnight came and went without anyone noticing; there were no strains of "Auld Lang Syne" in Monkswell Street that night.

It didn't take them long to put out the fire. All the buildings in the Close had smoke alarms and sprinkler systems installed long ago, so the fire brigade got there before too much damage had been done. But they stayed for hours, making sure all the sparks were out and nothing was going to spread. All the fire departments for miles around must have been there, including a number of volunteers. One, an old man, stood almost at attention by the sand buckets most of the night, his faded old eyes alert and his head held high, as he must have stood guarding his cathedral against fire during the war.

Most of us, less heroic, simply got in the way, or tried

to. We streamed, the whole party, down the street to the
gate, where the firemen politely but firmly refused to let
us into the Close. There wasn't much to see anyway. What
seemed like mass confusion, but was really very well-
organized fire fighting, kept us from getting more than a
glimpse of water and smoke.

I was doing my share of rubbernecking when Alan
caught up with me, firmly cut me out of the flock, and
herded me to my house.

"Please stay here," he said crisply, all traces of champagne and camaraderie gone from his voice. Chief
Constable Nesbitt was on the job. "I may need to use your
telephone from time to time. I'm going to have a word
with the fire chief now, and then the dean. I'll be back."

He dispersed the rest of the crowd with brisk courtesy
and then went about whatever it was he had to do. He
was in and out for an hour or more, making quick phone
calls full of jargon I couldn't understand. I brewed a pot
of coffee, and he snatched some now and again. Finally,
at about three, I suppose, he said he didn't need the
phone anymore and I should try to get some sleep.

That was easy for him to say; not so easy for me to do,
right there in the middle of the chaos. Lights were still
flashing through my bedroom window, and I could see
and hear lots of activity below.

Nor could I turn off my mind. How had the fire
started? The house was unoccupied. The canon's house-
keeper, I knew, was a daily who worked for several of the
bachelor clergy and staff; she didn't live in. The wiring
was sound in the house; the rewiring project on which the
cathedral was still engaged, at the insistence of the insur-
ance people, had been completed in the Close. It was just
possible that it had been improperly done at the canon's
house, but it seemed unlikely; it'd been thoroughly
checked.

So how had the fire started?

The question was answered soon after I awoke. I made coffee and fed Emmy, who had forgotten all about her early breakfast, and when I opened the door to let her out I found Alan standing on the step, his fist raised to knock.

"Come in and have something to eat," I said. I was glad I'd thrown on some clothes, but wished I'd taken time for my hair and some lipstick as well. "I just got up, so I'm not sure whether it'll be breakfast or lunch. Which would you prefer?" I closed the door after him, but he didn't come any farther than the hall.

"I can't stay," he said. "My driver's back on duty, and waiting for me. I have to be at headquarters at one o'clock, and before that—" He swept a pointing hand from his face to his feet, and I saw the evening clothes beneath his coat. His chin was bristly and his eyes bloodshot.

"Well, I appreciate formality in this casual age, but a dinner jacket at noon is overdoing it a bit, I agree. I suppose you never got to bed."

"Never got home. Mrs. Allenby kindly offered me a bed, and I slept very well."

"But not very long. You look terrible. Won't you have some coffee, anyway?"

"You pay such lovely compliments," he quoted. "One quick cup, perhaps, then I really must go." He followed me to the kitchen and I put a steaming cup in front of him.

"I stopped," he said, "because there are two pieces of news, bad news, but you'll want to know. The first is that the fire was definitely caused by arson."

"Oh, Lord! A firebug in the Cathedral Close? I knew it, though, really. How else could it have started?"

"Precisely. And the second is that a body was found in the house. Identification wasn't easy, but it seems pretty certain now that it was the verger, Robert Wallingford."

"Wallingford!" The wheels were turning furiously.

"That must mean he went over to the house to look for something, something incriminating, maybe, and—and either set the place on fire accidentally, looking around with a lighted candle or something, or did it on purpose to destroy the evidence and got caught in it himself!"

Alan smiled, if a trifle wearily. "All very sound deductions, Miss Marple. Except that you left out one vital fact. I don't blame you; you didn't know it. Neither did I until a few minutes ago when my people reported back."

He paused. I shook my head. "No clever guesses this morning. I haven't been awake long enough. Tell me."

"Wallingford was dead before the fire started. The details are unpleasant, but the condition of the lungs makes it certain. And the condition of the skull makes it almost certain that he was murdered."

"And the fire was started to conceal the fact," I put in.

Alan shrugged. "That, of course, is an inference. We're not making many of those at the moment. I should be on my way; I've asked the chief inspector in charge to report to me at one o'clock."

"You really like being a policeman, don't you?" I asked curiously. "Even when it means working on New Year's Day, and Christmas, and goodness knows when?"

"I like it when there's something to get one's teeth into. I detest it when it's one budget conference or committee meeting after another, or when one is tied up in red tape. Which is another thing I must deal with this afternoon; I have to sort out with the Fire Service just who is investigating what in this arson-cum-murder, and diplomacy is not my strong suit. Wish me luck."

"Will you let me give you supper?" I called as he got in the car. "Seven or so?" He nodded and was driven off.

That gave me the afternoon to fret about what I had in the house fit to feed a man who appeared to enjoy his food, and to ponder the question of this new friendship.

On the whole, I decided as I fussed about the kitchen,

it was pleasant to have a man noticing me, but more than a little unsettling. It had been so many years since I'd given a second thought to any man but Frank. We'd had such a *good* marriage that we hadn't needed many other people.

I was standing there with the refrigerator door open, staring unseeing, until I pulled myself together and focused on the turkey. Let's see, I had carrots, onions, potatoes—turkey potpie, then. Easy, filling, and good. It had been one of my favorites back home for post-holiday supper parties with close friends. Most of our friends had tended to be other couples, people we knew from church or our respective schools. When I'd found myself alone, they had been an enormous help at first, but had gradually drifted away as the weeks passed; they lived lives as couples, too, and I was an embarrassment.

That was one of the reasons I'd come to England, gone ahead with the plans Frank and I had made together. Here, where we'd known a number of unmarried people, I thought it might be a little easier to fit into the scheme of things.

I hadn't given a thought to finding a man. I didn't want any other man. I wasn't ready yet . . .

Ready for what? asked one of those inner voices. *You're acting as if he had proposed to you. Or propositioned you. He's lonely, and he likes talking to you, and that's all there is to it, so stop getting panicky.*

Which was such sensible advice that I took it, for once. I put my pie together to bake later, made a pumpkin cheesecake to go with it, and put a nice white wine in the fridge to chill in case Alan had a driver tonight.

Somewhat to my surprise, he arrived promptly at seven, neatly shaved and dressed and dropped off by a driver.

"Good," I said, opening the door. "That means you can have a drink. And I hope you can tell me at least part of what's happening; I'm dying by inches. The radio hasn't said a thing. Is scotch—I mean, whiskey, all right?"

"Actually, I developed a taste for bourbon when I spent some time in America, and I noticed the other evening that you stocked it."

"Jack Daniel's, my favorite. Good, I'll pour two. When were you in America?" I called from the kitchen.

He followed me. "Oh, several years ago now. The FBI ran a training session in terrorism, and asked me over to speak about the IRA. I spent two weeks in Washington, D.C., in August. I also learnt to drink ice-cold beer."

"Oh, dear, D.C. in summer is enough to make you appreciate the English climate, which is saying a lot. I haven't appreciated this winter a bit. I want some snow so badly, and instead we get frost and fog and sleet and rain, everything *but* snow. Shall we stay in the kitchen where it's comfortable? And I'll know when the pie is done."

"It smells very nice indeed, and this," he raised his glass, "is ambrosia."

I sipped mine. "Mmm, yes. Now, what can you tell me?"

"Well, for a start, you can be grateful for that despised rain. We've had so much of it the canon's house was quite damp; that's one thing that kept the fire from being much more serious."

"How was it started? Or maybe you can't say." I was determined not to get my knuckles rapped a second time.

Alan looked uncomfortable. "I haven't been very consistent about that sort of thing, I fear, Dorothy. But you see, you kept bringing up the subject when I wanted to talk about other things. And then I kept wondering if my instinct to trust you was being influenced by the fact that you're an attractive woman. I should have listened to my instinct. It's a good policeman's most valuable asset, and it's never let me down yet. So."

He tented his fingers. "The fire started in the fireplace

in the late canon's study. Apparently the arsonist put a
quantity of paper into the grate, doused it with lighter
fluid, and contrived a fuse of some sort."

"How on earth can they tell?" I interrupted. "The
whole point of lighter fluid is that it's volatile, so it would
be long gone, even the smell. And the container goes back
into a pocket; it isn't like gasoline, petrol, I mean."

"Well done. In fact, they wouldn't know, except that
whoever did it was careless. The arsonist left a tail of fluid
leading back out into the room, and that tail, crossing the
stone hearth to the hearth rug, ignited the rest. It leaves a
distinctive mark when it burns on something non-
flammable, you see, so the trail is clear. If he, or she—"

"I suppose we'll have to stick to one or the other. Let's
use 'he' for convenience' sake."

"So long as we don't forget that 'she' is just as likely.
There's no reason at all to suppose any of these crimes
couldn't have been committed by a woman."

This was a new idea. Inga? Greta? Good heavens, Jane?
I gave it up for the moment and simply nodded.

"If 'he,' then, had been more careful to squirt the fluid
in the grate and then around the rest of the room, leaving
no tails, even though the presumption of arson would still
be strong, it would probably be unprovable."

The timer went off. Alan put a salad together and
opened the wine while I laid out plates and set the steaming pie on the table. "That's all we're having," I said.
"Very simple."

"It looks excellent."

We ate single-mindedly for a few minutes, but when
the edge was off my hunger I pursued the arson. "What
clues would you have had to arson, with no tails?"

"Not I; the arson investigator. I'm not an expert in the
field, at all, but I do know that they can tell something
about the speed of the burning from the ash. Obviously if
something that one would expect to burn quite slowly,

such as a carpet, has in fact burnt very fast, the investigator wonders why. Dorothy, this is marvelous."

"Save some room for dessert. That's fascinating, about the fire. It's a wonder the whole place didn't go up."

"Without smoke detectors and the sprinkler system it might very well have done, even with the rain-soaked roof."

"And—the verger—"

"Please believe me, Dorothy, you don't want to know the details. I found them unpleasant enough and I'm used to these things. I will say only that they had to rely on dental records for identification."

"But how did they know where to look? I mean, you said yourself forensic evidence is no good without something to match it to, and everybody in Sherebury has teeth. Well, maybe not everybody. I suppose some sets get popped in a glass at night. But out of the whole population of the town that see dentists, how did they know to go to *Wallingford's* dentist to check the records?"

"That was another piece of carelessness. The murderer forgot to remove Wallingford's verger's badge, which survived the fire. So my men had only to check which of the vergers was missing. Simple."

I shuddered. Somehow that detail was especially poignant. The vergers were proud of their little brass lapel pins, and wore them with dignity. Wallingford, pompous ass though he was, had been proud of his, too.

Alan was watching me. "Dorothy, don't forget he never knew about the fire. He was dead before it started."

"Thank you, Alan. That does help. I was imagining . . ."

"Don't, is my advice. You said something about dessert?"

We worked our way through cheesecake and coffee and decided to take our brandy to the parlor; the kitchen chairs were getting a little hard. Alan made short work of building up a nice fire in the parlor grate.

"Alan, how did you get involved in police work?" I asked when we were nicely settled with some Mozart on the CD player. "It seems an odd career for a man like you."

He looked at me, amused. "And what am I like?"

"Oh—cultured, sensitive, observant, kind." I blushed a little. Was I getting too personal?

"You must admit that 'observant' is a pretty good qualification for a copper. You might have added inquisitive and self-righteous. I like to know what's going on, and I don't like crime. And I found that knowing a little about what people think and feel—there's your 'sensitive,' I suppose—made me good at the job. So I stuck with it. That's all, really."

"I can't imagine you enjoyed catching the crooks, when you did that personally. I mean actually arresting them and charging them with murder or whatever, especially back when you knew they might hang."

"No, it could sometimes be a nightmare. I used to wonder if I had the right, or if any man had the right, to take the life of another. But then I would think of the victim, whose body I had always seen, remember, and remind myself that he or she hadn't deserved to die, either. That helped. And there was a satisfaction about coming to the end of a case, knowing that one had taken a villain off the streets and freed everyone else from suspicion." He sipped his brandy, a little embarrassed about airing his feelings.

"I wish we'd come to the end of this one," I said fervently. "It seems to me we're right back where we started. We were so sure—well, I was, anyway—about Wallingford, and now he's been murdered, so obviously—"

"No, not quite obviously. Murderers have been murdered before now. But I agree, the probability is against it. I've been thinking a good deal today about the money he paid back to the cathedral." He paused to let that sink in.

"You think it was an admission of guilt? An atonement,

sort of? Or—no, of course, what an idiot I've been. Blackmail!"

"It does make one wonder, doesn't it? A murder is committed in or around the cathedral. A man who frequents the cathedral, and who lied about his actions on the night of the murder, is suddenly in possession of a large sum of money. Then he himself is murdered."

"He obviously never read Agatha Christie," I said flippantly. "She knew that blackmailing a murderer was a very dangerous way to make money."

Alan looked at me, cupped his glass in his hands, and looked away. "Dorothy," he said, gazing fixedly at the flames of the dying fire, "you'll resent this, I suppose, but you do realize that hunting down a murderer is also a hazardous occupation? I wish you'd leave it to us. I know you're intelligent and clever, and all the rest, but I do wish you'd give it up. It would—damage my pride considerably if you . . ." He didn't finish the sentence.

"No, I don't resent it, not now. It's very kind of you, really. But—I can't give it up, Alan. Not and ever live with myself."

"So long as you don't forget," he said with an edge to his voice, "that the operative word is 'live.'"

∽15∾

JANE POPPED HER head in the back door. "Dorothy? Going to market. Need anything?"

I seized the chance to get out of the house. "I'll come with you."

Jane was uncommunicative as we walked up the street.

"Beautiful day," I offered tentatively. "More like April than the second day of January. Although it seems unnatural to me; I really like winter to be winter."

Jane snorted.

"I suppose you've heard the news," I said after another moment or two of silence. "About Wallingford, I mean."

She grunted.

I presumed that was a yes. Well, whether she wanted to talk about it or not, I did. "But, Jane, it's important! If he didn't kill the canon, who did? They'll start looking cross-eyed at Nigel again!"

She grunted once more, and even spoke. "My house the whole time."

I got it after a beat or two. "I know Nigel was at the party when the fire started. No, he couldn't have done that. But the police aren't sure the two murders were committed by the same person. And everyone else who's in

the running for First Murderer was at the party, too. Jeremy
Sayers was playing the piano the whole evening, and Mr.
Pettifer was stuffing his face and holding forth about something most of the time. What was he doing there, by the
way, Jane? I didn't know he was a friend of yours."

Jane unbent at last. "He's not. Bag of wind, but he
never refuses an invitation. Wanted to talk to him about
that building scheme of his. Never got the chance."

"You may get the chance now," I pointed out as we
rounded the corner into the Market Square. "There he is."

He was strutting across the marketplace like a one-
man parade. Jane quickened her march to intercept him,
and timed it nicely, reaching his path just a second before
he did. He very nearly ran slap into her, which put him
off balance, literally and metaphorically.

"Morning, Councillor."

"Er—good morning, Miss Langland. I hope I didn't—
that is—I trust—"

I joined in gleefully. "Good morning, Mr. Pettifer.
Lovely morning, isn't it?"

He turned to me and raised his hat stiffly. "I'm afraid
you have the advantage of me, madam."

"Sorry," said Jane with a glint in her eye. "Mr. Pettifer,
my next-door neighbor Dorothy Martin. Dorothy found
the body."

"I beg your pardon?"

I put my hand out. "How do you do?" I said sweetly.
"Jane means that I was the one to find poor Canon
Billings."

"Oh—ah—indeed. Most unfortunate, most unfortunate. He will be sorely missed."

That was Jane's cue. "Miss him like a toothache yourself, eh?"

"I'm not sure that I understand you, Miss Langland."
The sun was still shining warmly, but the conversational
temperature was dropping fast.

"Hear you'll go ahead now with your slum program." Her wording left doubt as to whether Pettifer was going to tear down slums or build new ones. Or both. "Understand Billings was against it."

"My dear lady." He ignored me completely. My accent had placed me as an American, therefore a nonvoter and a person of no influence whatever. "It is by no means certain that the council will go ahead with *our* building program." He stressed the plural. "No, no, not at all certain. We shall have to consider all options most carefully. I should not wish you to believe that it is the habit of your Borough Council to engage in precipitate action. No, no, debate and compromise have made our great British system what it is. I will concede the likelihood that we shall now be able to conduct our deliberations without that attitude of stubborn obstruction to progress which characterized—" He suddenly remembered that he was supposed to be sorry about Billings's death. "That is, although Canon Billings was a most capable man, one cannot deny that he lived to a great extent in the past. Admirable in a scholar, no doubt, but a sad mistake for a practical man. If one lives in the past, I am fond of saying, one will never envision the future, and it is the vision of the future which makes for a vibrant present.

"Speaking of which"—he made a great show of consulting his watch—"my own future presses. I trust you will excuse me, ladies. Good morning."

"Should we have applauded?" I asked when he had raised his hat and gone.

Jane snorted.

I WAS STILL restless after putting away my purchases, and still trying to digest Mr. Pettifer's political address. A pretty unappetizing tidbit, really. If the man thought any more of himself he'd have trouble finding hats to fit.

But I thought, reluctantly, that I couldn't see him as a murderer. On the whole I thought he'd find very little that was worth a risk to his own precious skin. It was a pity, too, because that left the field, in my mind, to Jeremy Sayers and Nigel, with or without some of the Endicotts. All of whom I liked very much better than Mr. Archibald Pettifer. Goodness, how that man could talk without saying anything!

In fact, however, he had reintroduced one idea to my head. Billings, he'd said, had lived in the past. That was what I'd been chasing earlier: Just which part of the past was he living in before he died? No one seemed to know, and I remembered that I'd intended to ask George.

Well, what was wrong with right now?

The walk was altogether more pleasant than the last time in the fog. The morning really was delightful. A few plants were pushing green spikes through the ground, tulips and daffodils and crocuses. The jasmine creeping over garden walls was covered with tiny yellow flowers, and in the warmth of the sun the earth was beginning to smell like spring. And in the little parks I passed, the children contrived to make just as much noise and get just as muddy as they would when spring really did arrive.

In George's street his raw modern atrocity shone brightly in the sun, defiling the gentle, harmonious blend of gray stone and golden stone, tile roof and slate roof. I knocked for some time on his door before giving up.

Alice was probably doing the marketing, but I couldn't see George going along on such a woman's errand, as he would think of it. He seemed to have been spending a lot of time over the holidays at the university, though, working on his book. I toiled up the steep little hill to the campus.

Sherebury actually has a campus, if a small one, somewhat in the American pattern. It's a Victorian institution that has recently grown, so there's an odd mixture of old and new buildings, but that looks American, too. George's office was in one of the old buildings, I thought, but I'd only been there once or twice and wasn't sure I remembered which. I'd have to ask someone, though few students were around during the holidays.

I turned a corner, and there, against all the odds, I saw George, heading down a pathway. He was facing away from me, and by his side, attentively by his side, walked an extremely shapely girl in an extremely short skirt.

And suddenly Alan's remarks came back to me and I put two and two together with such force that I almost turned around in a panic and went home.

Oh, *no*! Not George! But if he was still playing tomcat, and if Billings knew about it and threatened to tell Alice, Alice with the money . . .

Rabbits, when threatened, freeze and try to become invisible. If they have to run, they run like the wind. But if they are finally cornered, they will fight. No one expects it, which makes them that much more dangerous.

What would George have done? Bluster, deny the whole thing, plead? Nothing would have been of any use. Billings would have been precise as to his facts, adamant in his attitude. And George, goaded beyond endurance, would have picked up whatever was handy, and . . .

As the imaginary blow fell, I shook myself. Common sense told me I couldn't condemn George for murder just because he was walking across the campus in broad daylight with a girl. There were a hundred innocent reasons for that, for heaven's sake. No, I came to talk to him, and I was going to talk to him. I'd have to trust my talent for prevarication to get me through without disaster. I took a deep breath and called out.

"George! Oh, George!"

The looks they gave each other as they spun around made me panic again. I saw her shoulders jerk with a quick intake of breath, saw the guilt in her round eyes.

George, on the other hand, looked quite simply furious, though whether at her for her obvious reaction or at me for my interruption, I couldn't tell.

I had no choice now but to ignore their distress and go through with it. I walked up to them, smiled at the white-faced girl, and turned to George.

"I'm so glad I caught you, George." Did they wince at my unfortunate choice of words? I hurried on. "I was out for a walk, and there's something I wanted to ask you. Are you terribly busy or could you spare me a few minutes?"

"Thank you ever so much for your help, Professor Chambers," said the girl, glancing from him to me like a nervous mouse. "I shan't take up any more of your time." She ran up the path.

"Did I interrupt something, George?" I asked pleasantly and, I realized too late, ambiguously.

He cleared his throat. "A—um—an undergraduate. Reading for one of my seminars. We were discussing—ah—"

I was as embarrassed as he. "Well, at any rate, now that I *have* interrupted, do you suppose you'd have time to talk to me? Just for a little while—in your office, if it's all right," I added firmly. "I've walked a long way and I'm not as young as I used to be."

He had little recourse but to consent, however ungraciously, and lead me to the cramped room in one of the older buildings that served as his office.

It was not only cramped, it was stuffy on this warm day, and a terrible mess. "Gracious, George, you've been neglecting your housekeeping," I said as I picked up a pile of papers from the only visitor's chair. "Is this your book? Where shall I put it?"

He grunted something and shoved a dented brass planter away from the corner of his desk. I put the papers in its place, hoping they wouldn't cascade onto the floor.

"That plant of yours could use some water," I commented idly.

He glanced at it, irritably. "Needs repotting. Haven't had time. Now, what was it you wanted, Dorothy? I don't mean to be rude, but . . ."

I sat down, fiddling with the plant while I considered an approach. "What it needs is a new pot. This one's had it. But I think the plant's dead, anyway."

Might as well go ahead and ask, now that I was here. "George, I won't be long, I promise. But I was glad to find you, because I did want to ask you about Canon Billings's book. I've been trying to find out what he was working on. No one seems to know anything except that it was about St. Paul. I thought, since that's more or less your field, too, he might have talked to you. Do you have any idea?"

George had taken his pipe from his pocket and was taking forever to light it, using his gadgety pipe lighter and sending small abortive puffs of sickeningly sweet smoke into the already airless room.

"What makes you think," puff, puff, "it was about," dig, wheeze, puff, "St. Paul?"

"I'm not sure, really—oh, yes, something the dean said. But he didn't know, he was just guessing."

The pipe seemed now to be going properly, to my regret. "I think he's wrong. Billings never said anything definite to me, but I got the distinct idea it had to do with Nero."

I blinked away the smoke. "Nero! Why on earth would he be interested in Nero?"

"Nero's connection with Corinth, you know. The canal he engineered across the peninsula. Didn't actually get built until this century." He puffed energetically, beginning to disappear in a blue haze. "Was there anything else? I am rather busy . . ."

I swallowed a cough. "No, thank you, George, sorry to

bother you. If you do get any firmer lead on what he might have been doing . . ."

"Not likely to, but I'll keep it in mind. Enjoy the lovely day, Dorothy."

I escaped, had a coughing fit in the corridor, and found my way outside, where I stood actively enjoying the pleasure of breathing.

∾16∾

THE MOMENT I got back I wanted to talk to Jane, but she wasn't home. It took some courage to go to the phone.

I succeeded on the third try.

"Chief Constable Nesbitt here."

He sounded so official I suddenly felt about ten years old. "Um—are you terribly busy? This is Dorothy Martin, and I have something to tell you, but if you're—"

"Yes, Mrs. Martin." His voice warmed slightly, but apparently we were going to be formal. "I'm sorry, I *am* late for a meeting; my driver is waiting. May I ring you up later, about seven perhaps?"

"Yes, of course, it's nothing urgent. Good-bye."

When the telephone rang a few minutes later I was sure his meeting had been canceled and he was on his way over. "Hello?" I said eagerly.

"Dorothy! My dear! We just got back, we've been in Paris, and we read all about the fire and *another* murder. Are you all right? Do you need any help? What can we do?"

"Lynn! You can't imagine how glad I am to hear from you. Actually, my urgent need right now is to talk to somebody, and you're exactly the person."

"That's why we called." Tom's voice came on the line.

"Lynn and I thought you might like to get out of that idyllic little village of yours, with all that boring peace and quiet, and there's a pub outside Maidstone we've been wanting you to see, anyway. Have you mastered the wrong side of the road yet, or shall we meet you at the train in Maidstone?"

I gulped. I had, in fact, learned to drive on the left, but the thought of doing so still left me weak-kneed. And those awful traffic circles they call roundabouts, with buses and trucks bearing down on you from the wrong direction . . . "Yes, of course, I'm all right as long as there isn't too much traffic," I lied staunchly. "I need really good directions, though, Tom. Every single roundabout I come to is going to have five ways out of it, to Little Puddleby, and Upper Slaughter, and Something Parva, and heaven knows what, and not one word about Maidstone, and I'll just keep driving round and round in circles . . ."

"Relax, kid. You know how to get from your house to the motorway, don't you? Toward London?"

"Certainly." I put on my dignity.

"Okay, then here's what you do . . ."

He made me write down every step of it.

"It sounds simple enough," I said dubiously.

"It's an easy hour from your house. If you haven't found us in an hour and a half, say by four-thirty, get to the nearest phone booth and call the Wicked Lady, and we'll come and find you." He gave me the number. "You still driving that beat-up old Beetle?"

"I'll have you know my VW is a perfectly reliable car. It does get a little cold in winter, I admit, but today's nice and warm. Besides, it's all that'll fit in my little afterthought of a garage."

"Hah! You just like it because the steering wheel's on the left, American style. Okay, we'll see you by four-thirty, right?"

"Right."

Halfway out the door I realized I wouldn't be home for Alan's call. Should I leave a message? I decided I should, but I kept it brief and formal. Mrs. Martin would be out for the evening but would try to reach Chief Constable Nesbitt in the morning. Thank you very much. I called for Emmy, but she had disappeared; very well, she could stay out until I got home. Serve her right. I was off.

I made two wrong turns and had one close encounter with a tow truck, but I made it. When I walked into the pub a little over an hour later, Tom and Lynn were waiting for me with a Jack Daniel's already poured.

"Ah, thank you, I need a little stiffening. But I daren't drink much. There's still the drive home."

"Don't worry." Tom patted my knee. "I'm having a pint and then switching to tonic so I can drive when we go eat. By the time you get behind the wheel again you'll be fine, with dinner and all."

"But Dorothy, what do you think of this place? We found it all by ourselves, we're so proud!" Lynn beamed. "And isn't the name luscious?"

"Delightful—the place and the name. There must be a story behind it."

"Oh, that's the best part. She really was a wicked lady. . . ."

Lynn and Tom told the story, interrupting each other and quarreling happily over the details. It was an unlikely tale of a lusty seventeenth-century matron-turned-highwayman, lady of the manor by day and, disguised as a man, robber by night. Some said she had died in this very pub, and within these walls it was easy to believe, easy to hear hoofbeats and the heavy rattle of coach wheels over cobblestones, with the wind echoing, "Stand and deliver!"

"Oh, that's perfect," I said with a luxurious sigh when they had finished. "And as Winston Churchill said about King Arthur and the Knights of the Round Table, it is all true, or it ought to be."

"Exactly!" said Lynn delightedly. "I believe every word of it, myself."

"All right, now, D., we brought you here to talk, and my lovely wife hasn't let you get a word in edgewise."

"Hah!" said Lynn. "Look who's calling the kettle black. But we're *dying* to hear all about it! First of all, *are* you all right?"

"Oh, I'm fine. At least, nobody's after me, if that's what you mean. But as a Sherlock Holmes, I'm beginning to think that I make a wonderful Watson."

"I knew it," said Lynn dramatically, pressing her hands together and rolling her eyes skyward. "I knew you were getting yourself mixed up in all this, I could feel it in my bones. What do you mean, Watson? You're a *"perfect* Mrs. Pollifax."

"Maybe I look the part. I realize I'm the only nonroyal woman in England who still wears hats. But I'm getting the clues all wrong. The most recent victim was my prime suspect."

"Yeah, well, that would create a little problem, wouldn't it?" said Tom, rubbing one ear. "Tell us about it."

I related my progress, or lack of it. It took me through another drink. "So now," I concluded, "I'm left with two suspects, neither of them with a very good motive, really. And they both have an alibi for the second murder, anyway. I suppose the police are looking into that. I'm going to talk to Alan about it tomorrow, I hope."

"Alan?" Lynn arched her eyebrows.

"The chief constable. We've gotten to be friends, so he's letting me in on some of what's going on. Now don't look at me like that. He's a friend, and that's all there is to it. And that's all I want right now."

One of the nicest things about Tom and Lynn is that they never carry a joke too far. Their agreement to drop the subject didn't even require an exchange of glances.

"So you're down to two suspects, huh? Sounds like

everybody in town wanted to do the guy in; there must be more than two."

"There is one more, actually. As of today. That's what I wanted to talk to you about. It's really very—distressing. You see, it's George Chambers."

"George!" Lynn's eyes widened, and Tom gave a long, low whistle.

"I know. I wouldn't have thought the White Rabbit would ever have the nerve, but—"

Tom choked on his tonic. "The *what*?"

"Oh, dear, I didn't mean to say that. And don't you go repeating it, it's private. It's just something about his hair—and his nose—"

"Don't. Stop," Tom wheezed. "You'll have us thrown out of here if I laugh any more. Oh, Lord, I'll never see him again without . . ." He wiped his eyes and blew his nose.

"One day," said Lynn when she could speak, "I will get even with you for that. Now tell, we are *panting* to know why you think the White Rabbit could possibly have had the backbone to murder anyone."

"It isn't very funny, really, except it's all rumor, and my imagination. Well, not quite all. I don't suppose, living way up there in your tight little London world, you've ever heard any stories about George playing around?"

"Good grief, D., that's not news!" said Tom. "Have you just caught on?"

"Alan says I'm naive," I admitted. "Or he said I was a nice woman, which amounts to the same thing. But when I went over to the university to talk to George today, I caught him with a coed. They were just walking along, talking, but they both looked awfully guilty when they saw me."

"And how does the occasional spot of adultery turn the poor old White Rabbit into a murderer?"

"That's where my imagination comes in. I thought, if

Alice doesn't know about it—and Billings knew—and he
threatened to tell Alice—"

"And Alice," Lynn concluded triumphantly, "would take
the money and run. George wouldn't be at all happy about
that; he enjoys the lifestyle to which he has become accustomed. Tacky as it is. Dorothy, you've been underestimating
yourself. I think you've *definitely* got something there."

"Yeah," said Tom. He didn't sound happy about it.
"An awful lot of guesswork, but you could be right. And
what do you do about it, my dear dimwit? You go trot-
ting over and ask him if he's a murderer!"

"Oh, come on, now. I'm not *quite* that stupid. I didn't
say a word about it. I just asked him what Billings was
working on when he died. I don't know why, but I'm
really curious about that, and I thought George might
know. He didn't, though. Or at least, he had a theory, but
it sounded awfully unlikely to me."

"Anyway, you'd better let that policeman pal of yours
know all about this right away. If you're right, the sooner
George knows that somebody else knows, the safer you
are. You done with that?" He gestured to my glass.
"Come on, doll, let's go to dinner."

"We're going somewhere else? The food here looks
very good."

"It is, Dorothy, but we've made a *real* find, a tiny place
that's three-star quality. The Old Bakehouse, over in
Rabbit's Cross."

"Appropriate," I murmured.

I probably would have behaved myself the rest of the
evening if the menu hadn't offered rabbit—well, lapin à la
something-or-other. When I saw it I started to giggle, and
then Tom realized why I was laughing and guffawed
himself, and I ended up with hiccups and suffered the
well-meaning suggestions of sure cures from everyone in
the place.

All in all we had a hilarious evening, exactly what I

needed. One never realizes quite how tight the strings are drawn until they are relaxed. As I drove home I felt better than I had in months, singing as I drove and negotiating the roundabouts with aplomb.

It was late, though, and I was so tired when I pulled the car into the garage that I nearly hit Emmy.

She was crouching in the middle of the concrete, lapping at something spilled on the floor. I left the car idling and got out to scold her and move her out of the way.

"What are you drinking, you little nuisance? Here, get away from that and let me see."

It was a greenish fluid that didn't look at all edible. I put a finger to it, smelled, hesitantly tasted. It had a slightly sweetish taste. Emmy struggled in my arms to get back at it, but I held her tightly and looked around, puzzled. I was sure I hadn't spilled anything out here, and it wasn't motor oil. Anyway the Beetle, old though it was, didn't leak oil.

And then I saw the can, tossed carelessly into a corner. I picked it up, smelled it, and was in the house in ten seconds and at the phone, an indignant cat still clutched in my arms.

Pray God the vet was there. He worked out of his home, so surely, at nearly midnight . . . he answered, his Scottish burr strongly in evidence.

"Two-seven-eight-two-four-r-r."

"Mr. Douglas? Thank God. I'm sorry, I know it's late, but—oh, this is Dorothy Martin."

"Yes. What is it?"

"It's Emmy. She's been drinking antifreeze, and I know it's supposed to be terribly poisonous—"

"How long ago?" His voice had changed from irritation to sharp anxiety.

"Just now. I came home and caught her at it. And I don't know how—"

"We'll talk about it later. Get her here, now!"

◈17◈

NOTHING IN SHEREBURY is very far from anything else. That night the three-minute drive to the vet's seemed to take an hour, Emmy howling in her carrier the whole way.

He met me at the door to his surgery. "I'm beginning to feel embarrassed about this, Mr. Douglas," I said as I tried to entice Emmy out of the box. She was growling, hissing, and employing all the weapons at her command—in short, acting completely normal. "She seems perfectly all right. Maybe she didn't get much, after all."

"Symptoms develop slowly. It's verra lucky ye saw her drinking it, ye ken; by the time the animal looks sick it's too late to save it. Ye're sure it was antifreeze?"

"I soaked it up with a sponge and brought it with me, just in case."

"Right."

That was the first faint sign of approval I'd gotten from him. I started to explain. "I can't imagine how she got into it. I never—"

"She's clever," he said brusquely. "This isn't going to be so verra pleasant. Perhaps ye'd best wait ootside."

He set down the soaked sponge and wrapped a thick towel firmly around the furiously angry cat, managing somehow to avoid teeth and claws. "Noo, then,

Esmeralda, ye'll no' care much for this, puir beastie." His voice was soft and caressing and melodious with the lilt of northern hills. Neither of them noticed when I left the room.

Tired as I was, I sat listlessly turning the pages of ancient magazines in the waiting room. Neither the wails coming from the next room nor my thoughts were conducive to sleep. Emmy was the healthiest-sounding sick cat I'd ever heard. Gradually the shrieks diminished, however, and I gathered Mr. Douglas had given her a sedative. The sounds that followed indicated various distressing occurrences. Emmy was evidently being purged of the poison.

Think about something else. Think about how in the world this could have happened.

Mr. Douglas hadn't let me talk about it. But then he didn't like a lot of talk. He was a Scot, and as dour and bleak as his native heath when he was with people. With animals he was kind and gentle and infinitely patient, perhaps because they didn't talk. Emmy loved him when they met socially, although at his office she felt she had to uphold the honor of her ancient race by vehement protests.

All the same, Mr. Douglas clearly thought my carelessness to blame for her present condition. The things he had so pointedly left unsaid were silent indictments. But the things I had tried to tell him exonerated me.

The point was, I didn't *have* any antifreeze. My beat-up old VW had an air-cooled engine. That's why the heater didn't work worth a hoot, and I froze in winter, but I didn't have to worry about the radiator doing the same. There wasn't one.

And even if I had a water-cooled car, I wasn't the mechanical type. I had my car serviced at a garage, where they fed it whatever mysterious fluids it required. Back home, Frank used to keep a little oil and antifreeze and

whatever around the house to top things up, but I knew
so little about the innards of a car that I never bothered.

Of course, my house was rented. Could there have
been a can of antifreeze left in the garage, overlooked?

That occupied me for another half hour, as I tried to
remember, and to shut out the sounds from the surgery,
but finally I shook my head. The house and garage had
been so clean when I moved in that I had been thoroughly
intimidated, knowing I could never keep things up to that
standard. I was quite sure there had been nothing at all in
the garage except a few gardening tools, spotlessly clean
and neatly hung from their proper hooks. No mess.

No antifreeze.

The surgery door opened, and Mr. Douglas beckoned.

"She'll do now," he said, stifling a yawn. "I've got the
stuff out of her and started her on an IV of ethanol."

"An IV of what?"

"Ethyl alcohol. Dr-r-rink." The rolled "r" made it
sound like an exotic potation. I must have looked doubt-
ful, for he launched into his lecturing mode, the only time
he ever uttered more than a few words.

"Antifreeze, ye'll understand, is ethylene glycol, a form
of alcohol. The body turns it to formaldehyde, and it pick-
les the internal organs and kills the wee beast. So we cast
it oot and give the patient charcoal to absorb the rest. But
even a bit left in the system is dangerous, so we make the
puir beastie drunk on ethanol. That drives oot the other,
ye see, and keeps it from doing its damage. We'll need to
keep her here twa, three days, until it's all oot of her system. She'll have a fierce hangover at the end of it all, puir
wee moggie. She'll no' like it, but she'll do."

He fixed me with a bleak gray eye. "Ye understand, do
ye, she'd have died if ye'd no' seen her drinking the stuff?
It's extremely dangerous, and I'll ask ye to be more careful
in future about leaving it about."

I couldn't let that pass. "Mr. Douglas, I'm more grateful

than I can say. Emmy is terribly important to me, and I don't know what I'd have done if . . . but you *must* understand. I didn't leave antifreeze where she could get into it. There's never been any at the house. I couldn't think about anything else, the whole time you've been with Emmy. I've been over it and over it, and *there was no antifreeze in that garage.*"

"Yon sponge was full of it," he retorted. "What are ye telling me, then?"

"I'm telling you someone put it there. You can think I'm crazy if you want to, but someone tried to poison Emmy."

His eyes grew even chillier. "And why would they do that?" Was the menace underlying his voice directed at me or an ostensible poisoner?

"How should I know how a poisoner's mind works?" I had an extremely good idea, but now was not the time to go into it. "Can I see Emmy now?"

"She's unconscious, but ye can see her."

She looked so small, stretched out on her side on the steel table. A section of her lovely thick fur had been shaved away for the IV needle, and the pale patch of skin looked cold. I stroked her head; there was no response.

"She—you're sure she'll be all right?" I swallowed and cleared my throat.

"Yon wee beastie's a fighter," he said, his accent broadening still further. "Ye'll no' need to worry. I've only had to sedate her because she wouldna let me treat her awake. Go home, noo. Rest. I'll ring ye in the morning. Not too airly." His voice had softened, and the hand on my shoulder, a gesture of sympathy and apology, told me he accepted my story. "And mind—I'd keep the door locked."

I did as I was told.

• • •

THE PHONE ROUSED me out of a deep but troubled sleep. I ran down the stairs, my heart pounding and my mouth dry. "Yes? Mr. Douglas?"

"Is that seven-three-two-double-four? Mrs. Dorothy Martin?"

I didn't recognize the voice; it must be his nurse. "Yes, this is Mrs. Martin."

"*One* moment, please, for Chief Constable Nesbitt."

I let out the breath I had been holding, and Alan, who came on the line immediately, heard me. "Did I catch you at a bad time, Dorothy? Should I ring up later?"

"No, I just thought you were someone else. I'm glad you called; I was going to call you. What time is it?"

"Eleven-thirty. I didn't wake you, did I? I thought you'd just be home from church."

"Oh, Lord, it's Sunday, isn't it? No, I didn't make it. I had—rather a bad night. Alan, I need to talk to you. You surely don't have meetings today, do you?"

"I'll be there immediately."

"Immediately" gave me just enough time to dress hastily and make a pot of coffee. Automatically I got out the cat food and looked around for Emmy. I was putting it back in the cupboard, with tears in my eyes, when the doorbell rang.

He noticed, of course; he's a good, observant policeman. "Dorothy, what's wrong?"

I gulped and tried to smile. "Nothing, really, I'm just being silly. She's going to be fine, but, oh, Alan, last night someone tried to poison Emmy!" My voice got a bit tight and I had to turn my head. "Would you like some coffee? I just made it."

He was understanding enough not to follow me into the kitchen, and by the time I got back with two cups I had myself under control.

"Right. Tell me about it."

I told him, careful to keep to the facts, while he drank

his coffee. "And they have to keep her full of the ethanol for a while, but she should be all right," I concluded.

"Good." He tented his fingers. "You're quite sure you had no antifreeze about?"

"Quite sure."

"And I gather you think you know who was responsible."

"I'm practically sure it was George Chambers." I laid down my line of reasoning about George and the canon once more. "I know it sounds awfully thin and iffy. But the fact is, I went to see George and caught him with a girl—and then Emmy was poisoned. Why would anybody do that, except to upset me and get me to shut up and quiet down for a while? George knows how much I love that cat; he'd know how devastated I would be if she died. He meant her to die, Alan. But the final touch is that anybody who knew about cars would know a VW Beetle doesn't use antifreeze, and George isn't mechanical. I think it makes sense."

Alan was silent, tapping his fingertips together. When he spoke, it was decisively. "I agree. There's no proof, but it deserves investigation. Did you touch the tin of antifreeze?"

"Yes, I picked it up. Sorry. A good thing you have my fingerprints."

"Right. I'll notify the DCI—sorry, detective chief inspector in charge of the case—and he'll send someone to pick up the tin and check the garage. Don't touch anything else, meanwhile. I'll suggest an interview with both the Chamberses. I should have thought of this myself. And, Dorothy, I know you hate being told what to do, but will you please for once stay home with your doors locked? This time it was your cat. The next time it will be you."

"I know. I'll behave. I have to see Emmy, and I badly need to go to Evensong, but I'll go straight there and back and not talk to anybody, I promise. I'm a little scared, I admit." I was terrified, but I had my pride. "Funny. I never thought I could be afraid of poor old George."

"It may not *be* Chambers, don't forget. Will you really be all right? I haven't a man to spare, or I'd give you some protection."

The idea of a policeman at my side made me laugh a little. "No, I'll be careful."

"I must go. Ring up at once if you feel uneasy about anything. If you can't reach me, ask them to send a constable."

I promised, feeling distinctly less safe as his reassuring presence disappeared into the police car.

I called Mr. Douglas and got his starchy assistant.

"Esmeralda is doing as well as can be expected, Mrs. Martin," she said with a sniff. "Mr. Douglas is monitoring her condition carefully. She is of course quite groggy. The treatment—"

"I know about the treatment," I interrupted. "But she really is all right? He said he would call me, and I was afraid . . ."

"Mr. Douglas has another emergency this morning, and is of course rather tired after a late night. It *is* a Sunday, after all." Her voice held volumes of resentment about working on her day of rest. "Your cat will be quite all right, but you *must* be more careful about antifreeze."

He hadn't told her, then. Good. I should have asked him to keep quiet about my suspicions, but evidently his own good sense had prevailed. It was better for the nurse to blame me, and I didn't mind a scolding so long as Emmy was getting better. "Thank you," I said meekly. "I'll look in on her this afternoon." I hung up before she could launch into how some people really shouldn't be allowed to keep pets.

After a sketchy lunch and a brief, troubled nap, I gave the details and the antifreeze tin to the polite young

sergeant who came around, and then set out by foot on
my errands, looking over my shoulder the whole way.
The clouds had moved back in, and it seemed to be getting colder and darker by the minute. Between cold and
nerves, I was nearly running when I reached Mr.
Douglas's office.

I was eager to see Emmy, but she didn't care at all
about seeing me. She was conscious, but only just. Mr.
Douglas had been accurate about her state of intoxication.
Her eyes didn't exactly focus; indeed they were slightly
crossed. She tried to get to her feet, and then gave up and
just sort of fell over, slowly. I've seen Skid Row bums
who looked more respectable.

At least she seemed to be progressing nicely. The
starchy nurse said something about monitoring her crys-
tal output, and although I didn't follow the details, the
news seemed to be good. I meekly accepted the lecture
she felt obliged to deliver and finally escaped, a bit com-
forted. At the rate things were going, I would have my
friend back soon. With a terrible headache, true, but
home.

Evensong was comforting, too. I sat by Jane. One of
her greatest virtues is that she doesn't talk when you need
quiet. The hymns were all Christmas lullabies, the anthem
Berlioz's lovely "Thou Must Leave Thy Lowly Dwelling,"
soft and lilting and gentle.

I sat listening and thinking about Jeremy Sayers up in
his organ loft, playing magnificently and directing the
choir with his head and an occasional wave of the hand.
Could a man who produced such glorious music be a
murderer? That was specious reasoning, I realized, but all
the same I was glad Jeremy's guilt seemed less and less
likely. George, on the other hand, an old—well, acquain-
tance, at least—I didn't like the idea of him as villain
much better. Did that get me back to Mr. Pettifer, who
was a prize ass, but . . . ? I shifted uneasily. I didn't want

to think about suspects, or crime, or wickedness. Was there never to be an end to the ripples of disorder and misery and evil spreading from the act of murder?

The readings provided, if not an answer, at least a comfort. One was from Romans, St. Paul at his most triumphant and reassuring: ". . . neither death, nor life, nor angels, nor principalities, nor powers . . . shall be able to separate us from the love of God . . ."

With those rolling cadences in my ears and Jane walking in sturdy silence beside me, I reached home in safety and fell into bed without another thought.

◎ 18 ◎

I WAS IN the middle of a very large breakfast, having eaten almost nothing the day before, when Alan called.

"Good morning, Dorothy. How is Esmeralda?"

Bless his heart! "Drunk as a skunk, but improving, they tell me. I saw her yesterday afternoon; you would have arrested her on the spot for public intoxication."

"You sound somewhat improved, as well."

"Yes, thank you. Have you found out anything?"

"There's been some progress. Will you be at home this afternoon? I'd like to fill you in."

"Any time, I have no plans."

After breakfast, seized with energy, I scurried about the house, tidying up, sweeping away masses of cat hair that would soon, I hoped, be replaced. Alan was right; I did feel better. Was it just a good night's sleep, I wondered as I vigorously scrubbed the kitchen floor. I hadn't felt this ambitious in weeks. It certainly couldn't be the weather, which was of that variety known to the romantic novelists as "lowering."

It wasn't until I sank down for a tea break that I identified the source of my animation.

I was angry.

In fact, I was furious.

The fine fury kept me warm all the way to the vet's office. All the same, I kept my wits about me as I marched through the narrow streets. They were crowded, and my heart beat a little faster every time someone jostled me, although I told myself not to be silly. This was Shrebury, not New York. I wasn't apt to be mugged in broad daylight on the High Street. No, the menace (I didn't try to pretend there was no menace) would strike more subtly, in the isolated dark, when I was alone.

Emmy seemed a little less uncoordinated; she licked my hand before swaying back into her stupor. This time I got to see Mr. Douglas.

"Aye, she'll do," he said briefly, showing me the back of his hand, bright with four parallel red lines. "Defended herself when I last examined her. She can go home tomorrow." He lowered his voice. "Ye'll be careful?"

I assured him that I would, indeed, be careful, and went home with a light step. I was getting my Emmy back!

I invited myself to Jane's for lunch. She was alone, for which I was grateful.

"Sorry to hear about Esmeralda, Dorothy," she said gruffly as she set out bread and cheese and various party leftovers. I didn't ask how she had heard; the Shrebury grapevine was at it again.

"She's coming home tomorrow, though. I just saw her, and she's well enough to scratch the doctor, poor man. But Jane,"—my hands had tightened into fists; I relaxed them—"whoever did this is going to get what's coming to him!"

She nodded soberly. "Worse when it's an animal, isn't it?"

"Every time. I suppose that's all wrong. It ought to be more important that two men have been killed. It *is* more important, of course. But there are reasons why people kill people—not excuses, but reasons, motives. When it's an innocent animal that never harmed anyone—" My hands clenched again; I changed the subject. "Where's Nigel?"

"Off hunting out a place to live. The dean gave him his job back, and a rise in pay, and he's as pleased as a dog with two tails."

"Jane, that's wonderful! But you'll miss him."

She shrugged. "Needs his independence. Have everything you need there?"

With mouth full, I nodded. She sat down and helped herself to some salad.

"What're you doing about it?"

"Not much yet. Alan Nesbitt is coming over this afternoon to tell me what he's found out, or I guess what his men have found out. I keep forgetting he doesn't go around investigating things himself. Jane, I—I have an awful feeling it's George Chambers."

"Mmm." She chewed slowly, thinking. "If Billings found out about his fancying the students, you mean."

"Yes. What do you think?"

"Don't know. Nesbitt will find out."

"That's exactly why I can't do anything until I talk to him. But I've more or less run out of other suspects. At least neither Jeremy Sayers nor Archibald Pettifer could have set the fire; they were both here the whole time. And it must have been the same person, don't you think?"

"Likely. Could be anybody."

With that we were back where we started more than a week before.

When Alan showed up at my door the cathedral change ringers were at their weekly practice, and with thick clouds almost touching the bell tower, the racket was even louder than usual.

"Whew!" Alan whistled once he was inside, with the sound muffled a bit. "How do you keep your sanity?"

"I've gotten used to it. I rather like it, to tell the truth, except when I've got a headache. Would you like some tea?"

"No, thanks, I've only just finished lunch, and I've a meeting in half an hour. I thought you'd want to be brought up to date, and the telephone is a trifle public."

"Well, sit down, anyway. It may be your one chance to sit in this house without getting yourself upholstered in cat hair."

"Indeed." He settled in my biggest chair and tented his fingers. "I have, as in the classic American joke, some good news for you, and some bad news."

"All right, I'll bite. What's the good news?"

"I hope you'll think it good news that we have, at least provisionally, eliminated George Chambers's motive."

Whatever I had expected, it wasn't that. "But I saw for myself—"

"I don't doubt what you saw, and you're quite right. Everything my men have gathered supports the view that Chambers is a confirmed womanizer. But we also interviewed Mrs. Chambers, separately, of course."

"And?"

"And she knows all about it. Has for years."

"But—I can't imagine her putting up with—"

"I didn't talk to her myself. But my DCI is a very competent chap with quite an understanding of psychology. He gained the impression that Mrs. Chambers views her husband with a kind of affectionate mockery and considers his affairs to be essentially harmless. She discussed the matter quite openly; there was no doubt that she knows, and, more to the point, that Chambers knows she knows."

"But—" I ran my fingers through my hair. "But then nothing makes sense. Why did somebody try to kill my cat, if it wasn't George putting me off the scent? Why—what did George say?"

"That's quite interesting. The DCI says he was distinctly

nervous, but not about the sex involvement. John told me Chambers was terrified when he walked into his office. He tried to put the man at ease by talking a bit about the book—it was scattered about everywhere—but it didn't help. The moment they got on the subject of the women, Chambers relaxed. John left feeling he should have asked something else, but he couldn't think what."

"Then I give up. No, I don't, but I don't know where to go from here. Does George have an alibi for earlier on New Year's Eve, the fire?"

"He says he was working on the book until he came to the party, where we both saw him. No one to verify the earlier time. The arson man says, with a very slow fuse, he might have had time to touch it off and still get home and back to the party before the flames started. Same thing for Christmas Eve, and for Saturday night when the trap was set for Esmeralda; working on the book, no witnesses. Pettifer and Sayers, we both know, have alibis for New Year's Eve, and Sayers for most of Christmas Eve— oh, yes, we've had our eye on them, too. Young Evans seems pretty well out of it, so far as we can verify his Christmas Eve story, and we never seriously considered the Endicotts; they're far too busy at night to be up to much mischief."

"So we're out of suspects."

"That, of course, is the bad news. We may not be precisely 'out of' them, but the best ones are looking less and less likely. And that means, Dorothy, that you will have to be even more on your guard; it could be anyone. I suppose it's no good asking you again to give it up?"

"No good at all. I'm sorry, Alan, but I love Emmy and I can't let someone hurt her without doing something about it. I don't expect you to agree with me."

He sighed. "I had a dog once, a year or two after Helen died. A beautiful golden retriever. Someone shot it while I was investigating a big robbery, I never knew for certain who. I haven't owned an animal since, but I do understand. Please take care."

The bells were still ringing gaily when he left.

So we were back where we started. No, worse; we had eliminated a lot of possibilities and knew less than nothing.

Hercule Poirot always says the solution to the crime lies with the victim. Find out enough about the character and activities of the murderee and it will inevitably lead to the murderer. Well, I'd found out a lot about Billings's character and it hadn't led anywhere useful. As to his activity—drat! I had forgotten to ask Alan if he had found out anything about Billings's unfinished work. I mulled over what Charles Lambert had said that day at the British Museum. It was odd, really, that Billings should have been so cagey about his work. It didn't seem characteristic.

Poirot always jumped on the uncharacteristic.

All right, why had Billings been so secretive? Did he think someone would steal his work? Nonsense; what would it have mattered if someone did? He wasn't an academic caught in the "publish or perish" syndrome.

He'd just been to Greece. Corinth, the dean had said. Did that have anything to do with it? Could he—oh, good grief, could he have stolen something from the museum in Corinth to work on here? That would urge discretion, all right, but it didn't sound likely.

Corinth. Corinthians. St. Paul. The Cathedral Church of St. Peter and St. Paul. St. Peter was going to be jealous.

Oh, dear God in heaven.

I suddenly saw it all, and I was scared stiff.

Confirmation. I needed confirmation. My hands shook as I reached for the phone.

I got the British Museum on the first try, but it took me forever to reach Charles Lambert. I was told it was not their policy to call readers to the telephone, and I finally had to say I was secretary to the chief constable of Sherebury. I hoped Alan would forgive me.

"Hello, Charles? Thank God! It's Dorothy Martin. Listen, Charles, this is terribly important. What was the book Jonathan Billings wanted to take away from you that day? Remember, the one you told me about?"

"I don't recall the name, Dorothy. I can look it up. Why, what's the matter?" He was infuriatingly calm.

"Never mind, what was it about?"

This time his answer came promptly. "The Dead Sea Scrolls—the methods they used to unroll and preserve them. Are you going to tell me what this is about?"

"Yes, but not now. *Thank you*, Charles!"

My second call was to Jane. "Jane, I can't explain now, but exactly what is George's book about?"

"The lost letter to the Corinthians, of course. St. Paul's other letter. You knew that; George talks about nothing else. He thinks he's proved it never existed."

Yes, I'd known it, but I'd never really listened. Well, there was my confirmation.

I changed into dark clothes and an old pair of what I still call sneakers, the better to do a spot of burglary. I was still struggling into my coat and hat as I headed out the door for the cathedral.

It never even occurred to me to call Alan.

◈19◈

IT HAD TO be there, I told myself as I raced through the Close. It had to be. It couldn't have burned up in the canon's house. Oh, please, God, let it be there!

Had the police searched the cathedral library? Probably. They were very thorough. But they wouldn't have known what they were looking for. Besides, did they read ancient Greek?

The library would be locked, of course. I would have to think of some reason to get in. Or, no, Nigel had his job back. He would be there, if he'd finished his flat hunting. Good, he could help me look.

But he wasn't there. I was out of breath by the time I reached the gloomy corner of the far transept, where the library dwelt in what used to be the chapter house. I tried to quiet my gasps; I felt strongly the need for caution, without being quite sure why.

The door was shut, but unlocked. Easing up the old iron latch cautiously, I pushed the heavy oak door open to the smallest possible slit I could get through. For a wonder, the hinges didn't creak. My heart beat so hard I could hear it; I hoped my arteries were in good shape. Too late now to wish I'd eaten fewer tea cakes in my lifetime. I closed the door behind me, leaned back against its firm panels, and took a deep breath.

The vast circular room was supported by a single central pillar. Bookcases stretching nearly to the lofty fan-vaulted ceiling lined the walls and pushed, spokelike, from the walls toward the center of the room, allowing only narrow aisles for access. Around the central pillar, desks and catalogue chests were set in a ring. The room was shadowy on even the brightest of days, the light from high windows losing heart amid all those dark surfaces. On this gloomy winter day the whole room brooded in obscurity. I considered finding the light switch and rejected the idea. Gloom suited my purposes nicely.

Where was I to start? He could have put it anywhere. A scroll to begin with, it would probably be flattened out now and sealed between sheets of glass or plastic. It could be anywhere among all these thousands of books.

Helplessly I looked about me. The big desk, the obvious place to start, looked depressingly clean, as though it had been tidied after Billings's death.

Well, I had to begin somewhere. And I didn't have all the time in the world. Someone might come in at any moment, and what I intended to do was almost certainly illegal. Praying for privacy, I tiptoed to the desk.

It was the movement that caught my eye. Deep in one shadowed recess between rows of shelves, a form raised a hand and took a flat folder from a shelf. As I watched, suddenly frozen as still as the marble pillar, the hooded monk glanced through the contents and replaced the folder on the shelf. The figure moved again, stooped to a lower shelf deep in the corner, and picked up something that shimmered a little with sullen light.

Fear and curiosity battled for precedence. I couldn't see what he was doing. He seemed absorbed in something and, thank heaven, oblivious to my presence. If he was a ghost, he was behaving rather strangely; if a man, what was he doing here in the dark, dressed like that?

Well, a ghost couldn't harm me, and in either case I simply had to see a little better. With infinite care I moved around the pillar, close to the head of the aisle where the dim figure stood.

Now I could see. He—it—stood close to the wall holding something up to what little light there was. Something that looked like a picture without a frame, stiff and shiny. I caught a reflection. Glass? Glass with—yes, two pieces of glass with something between them. My stomach clenched; I thought for a moment I would be sick. As I strained a little closer, my elbow caught the edge of a paper lying on the catalogue chest. It fluttered to the floor with a little sigh, and the sound undid me.

The figure turned toward me with a sharp hiss, and the hood fell back from his face. Even in the dim light I could see, too late, that he was no ghost.

"Hello, George," I said, moistening lips gone dry. "Going to a costume party?"

He laughed. The sound conveyed no humor at all. "You mean the habit? No, no, just a little joke. I've had some fun playing about with this in the cathedral. Scared some of the fools who believe in that old story."

"So it was you, that day in the clerestory. And at the library door, and at the restoration service?"

George had moved close enough that I could see the look of puzzlement on his face. "I don't know what you mean. I've never attended a service dressed like this. Wouldn't be right. Here, yes. And I went up to the clerestory level a few days ago, but it's called a triforium, you know, that walkway. Gave a few tourists a thrill. Were you there, then?"

"Yes," I said shortly. "You frightened me half to death. But George, I saw you later, too, when the dean and the bishop reconsecrated the side chapel. I suppose they'll have to do it again," I added parenthetically, "now that Wallingford has been killed."

"I tell you I don't know what you're talking about," George insisted. "But what on earth are you doing here?"

I tried to think fast. "That's just what I was about to ask you, George," I said, playing for time. "Surely not working, all in the dark. What's that you've found? May I see?" I edged toward the door as George moved closer.

"Oh, I don't think you would be interested, m'dear," he said in honeyed tones. He moved forward and picked up a large brass paperweight from the desk, toying with it. "Just an old manuscript. Been here for years, probably."

"I'd like to see, really, George." Oh, how I wanted to see! It was small to be of such shattering importance, about the size of a sheet from a legal pad, and closely written. Even though I couldn't read a word of Greek, just to see it, touch it. . . . "Don't be selfish, now!" I put out my hand, still backing as unobtrusively as possible toward the door. If only I could get my hands on it! I tried what I hoped was a sweetly sincere smile. "You know I'm so interested in your research!"

"My research!" George snorted. "What makes you think this is part of my research? Just something I found in the library just now. Of no importance, really." But he held the manuscript clasped firmly under one arm.

I stopped. It would have been better the other way, but if I could startle him into a sudden move there might still be hope. "George." I tried to make my voice quiet and reasonable and nannylike. "I know what it is. Hadn't you better put it down? What if you dropped it? You can't want that." What did he plan to do with that paperweight?

George stopped too. A wary look came into his eyes, but he played out the bluff. "Nonsense! Don't know myself what it is. Just a cathedral record of some kind, Middle Ages, probably. Parchment, you can see."

I shook my head wearily. There was no more point in fencing. "No, George. We both know that isn't true. It isn't parchment, it's papyrus. That's the letter, George. The one you've been looking for, dressed up like that, I suppose, so people wouldn't stop and question you. It's the one you say in your book doesn't exist, the lost letter from St. Paul that Canon Billings found in that earthquake in Corinth. The one you murdered him for."

The shock that had been growing in George's face turned to rage. He made a convulsive movement and tripped on the hem of his monk's robe, and that gave me just the moment's respite I needed. I dove for the chapter-house door and escaped, George at my heels.

I ran toward the choir, without plan, seeking light and people. There had to be someone about, someone who could help. I had the advantage for the moment; my sneakers and slacks made running easy. George in his robe and sandals was having a harder time of it, stepping on the hem and stubbing his sandaled toes on irregular paving stones.

There was no one at all in the choir. Turning my head frantically, I saw a staircase I'd never noticed, apparently leading to the organ loft. George was still around the corner. If I could get up there and hide . . .

There was no other way. If I screamed for help he'd get to me first. He'd think to tuck up his robe soon, or pull it off, and with his longer legs he'd catch up with me if I tried to run very far. Winded, my heart trying to thump its way out of my chest, I climbed the stairs.

It should have worked. I crouched behind the carved oak railings and peered down into the choir. He wasn't far behind me, but he guessed wrong and, after a quick glance around the deserted choir, started out into the nave. I moved cautiously to the other side of the cramped, dusty space and tried to look between the organ pipes to the crossing far below. The view was narrow and

restricted, and I couldn't see straight down, but after a
time I saw George, and what I saw appalled me. The
nave, too, was strangely empty. After a searching look in
all directions, George deliberately approached the crossing altar where four candles burned in their massive
holders. As calmly as in a lecture-room demonstration,
he took a pocketknife from under the robe and slit the
tape on three sides of the glass sandwich he held.
Folding the top glass back on the fourth-side hinge, he
took out the priceless manuscript and held it out toward
one of the candles.

He couldn't quite reach it, and stretched farther. My
foreshortened view distorted my perception, and I
couldn't tell by how much the fragile piece of papyrus
failed to reach the flame. Was it a foot, or an inch?
George laid the glass on the floor and tried again, and I
betrayed myself. Without conscious volition, I groaned
and uttered a tiny, anguished "No!"

I don't think I could have helped it, but it was a terrible
mistake. Quiet as it had been, it echoed round the nave,
resounding brassily from the organ pipes. George looked
up, and, as surely as if we had changed places, I saw him
catch a glimpse of my bright orange hat.

"Ah, there you are," he said softly. I ducked and
searched desperately for a way out.

I saw only one possibility. The current restoration
work on the two great piers to the south of the crossing
involved a scaffolding. If I could reach it and somehow
climb over the edge of the choir screen, perhaps I could
reach the other side and the triforium, which was also
under reconstruction and unused. I could then get down
by another stair. At the west end, preferably, where I
could run out into the open. Away from this place.

It was impossible, of course. The scaffolding was at
least two feet beyond the far corner of the choir screen,
and there were organ pipes in between, and carved wood

and stone. And I was feeling my age as I hadn't in months. I couldn't do it.

George's feet sounded on the curved stair to the loft. My own feet, moving without orders from their mistress, scrambled over the pipes and the carving, reached the corner, and mounted the railing.

It was carved in great stone fleurs-de-lis, excruciatingly uncomfortable. Straddling the railing, I looked down—once. Then I hugged the nearest piece of carving. My arms gripped so hard that the marble bit into my flesh, and I nearly cried out again.

He was in the loft now, moving very quietly, but I could hear a board creak now and again. The sound was getting closer. I dared not look around, dared not move.

And then George stumbled into the pipes and set up a fearful clatter, disturbing a mouse. In panic it ran over my foot, and the smaller fear blessedly delivered me from the larger. Shuddering, I left the safety of my railing and launched myself at the frail pipe work of the scaffolding.

My sneakers saved me. Leather shoes would have lost their grip, but the ribbed rubber soles grabbed and held just long enough for my arms to encircle a pipe, and then I was sliding down, down, for what seemed like an eternity until one foot struck a cross member, and I was caught, hanging crazily from the pipes, but safe for the moment.

In fact my position was much better, for I was close to the ladder. By stretching a little I could reach it with one foot, then a hand, then the other hand and the last foot. Ah! I could go where I liked now.

At least I could if I could get my shaking legs to move at all. How ridiculous it was for a woman my age to attempt this kind of exercise when I was so out of shape. With the tendency to the trivial of a mind at the last reaches of stress, I resolved firmly to lose some weight and start walking regularly.

If I survived. I considered the position. Up or down?
With all the noise he was making among the organ pipes,
George hadn't heard my terrified leap, so I had the choice.
Down meant people, in theory, and help. But there were
no people to be seen, and down also meant that huge
empty nave, with no place to hide. There was the south
transept, though. I could go out that door, if I got lucky,
and the clutter of tombs and chantries provided concealment if necessary. I moved down one rung, then another,
looked down for a moment, and saw George, now without his robe, emerging once more from the choir into the
nave. He had given up on the organ loft and was looking
elsewhere.

I went up. Very quietly.

My move across to the triforium railing was nasty, but
not so bad as the leap from the organ loft. The scaffolding
was much closer to that side, for one thing, and there was
only a board where the old railing used to be. It was relatively easy to climb around and over, and then I was in
the dark, littered triforium. Now I had to find a stair.

There was one in the corner, leading down to the south
aisle. That was out of the question, with George so close.
The west end, then. Was there a stair there? I didn't know,
but it seemed likely, and anyway I had no choice.

I was halfway along when I heard the crunch of his
feet in the litter of sawdust and stone fragments on the
floor. I froze behind a section of carved railing propped
up against the wall. I would make just as much noise as
he if I tried to move.

He came closer. "You have to be up here, Dorothy," he
said quietly, casually. "There's nowhere else for you to
have gone. And you'll have to come back this way. You
can't get down at the other end, you know."

That might be true and it might not. I stayed where I
was, and George came closer.

"You can't possibly get away, you know. And you do

understand why I have to kill you. I'm sorry about that, Dorothy. I tried to distract you, but you persisted. You'd ruin my book, all my chances. You'd tell them about the letter. You have to be destroyed, just as it does. I wanted to keep it, of course. Pity. Perhaps I'll go to Corinth one day and try to find more."

He was moving all the while, slowly, searchingly. He was—here. Perhaps he would go on past, get far enough away that I could make it to the southeast stair before he caught up with me. I tensed, ready to turn and run, but his footsteps stopped. I closed my eyes, afraid my stare would somehow attract his, until I felt his hand touch mine. . . .

"May I help you up?"

I stood, unsteadily. We were very quiet.

"George. There is a way out of this. Tell them about the manuscript. Tell them you found it, and you realize you were wrong. Write a new book; it will be even better."

It was foolish, and I knew it was. George knew it too. He took the paperweight out of his pocket. It was very large, with sharp corners.

"And what about murder, m'dear? Shall I tell them about that, too? Our beloved canon, who wouldn't wait to tell the world about his wonderful discovery until my book came out, and I had the Clarendon Chair? It would have been all right then. Can't blame a man for making a mistake when all the evidence isn't in. But he wouldn't do it. He was going to tell the dean. Came out to my office on Christmas Eve to tell me first; scholarly courtesy, he called it, but he came to sneer at me. 'I've actually found it, you see. I have it, in my possession. Of course you can't publish your book now.' I saw red. Pleaded with him first, and then I picked up that big brass flowerpot, and. . ."

"Why did you bring his body back to the cathedral, though?" Keep him talking; I might think of something.

"Had to get it away from my office, didn't I? Planned to leave it in his house, but his cleaner was still there, so I came across the Close, used his key, and slipped him inside the door." The man preened himself.

"And Wallingford?" I said quietly. I looked at the distance between us and the railing. Could I slip past, if I could distract him for a moment?

"He heard something Billings said to the dean, and put two and two together. First time in his stupid life he ever got a sum right. Blackmailed me on the strength of it, right here in the cathedral, and used the money to buy his way out of his own trouble. Shameful. Fool enough to turn his back on me, though. Of course I had planned to burn down Billings's house, to destroy any notes he might have made; it was brilliant, I thought, to put Wallingford's body in the fire. Just bad luck the fire was found so quickly."

And Emmy? I thought that, but didn't say it; I knew the answer to that one. I had the right man all along, but the wrong motive. I'd seen that dented pot on his desk and that frightened him badly, that and his book—though I hadn't understood about the pot, nor read a page of the book. And for that he nearly killed my cat. I thought of her lying there on the cold steel table; soft and still and helpless, and the thought gave me my anger back, and my courage. I fixed my eyes on the crossing altar, said a quick prayer, and screamed, "Dean! Help!"

It worked. George turned, startled, and I ran like a deer, coat flapping, hat askew. It was only a tiny chance. George was as out of shape as I, but his legs were longer, and he had the strength of desperation. I was nearly at the stair when I tripped, and went down, and in one last urgent attempt I picked up a piece of masonry and threw it.

It fell just ahead of George. But in swerving to avoid it, he struck the side railing, hard. The single, temporary plank held, but it bowed out and George missed his footing. Scraps of stone fell to the floor of the nave, forty feet below. He swore, scrabbled, grasped the plank once more.

This time it broke, with all his weight against it. As he fell, screaming, he clutched the manuscript fiercely with both hands, as if it could provide a handhold. It crumbled to bits. As I watched, paralyzed, the one large piece drifted down to a candle of the crossing altar and then, burning, wafted to the floor to join its destroyer.

THE DEAN WAS there, speechless with horror. Nigel was there. The police were there. Alan was there, finally, mercifully, to cut short the questions and explanations and let me go home. I didn't want any company. Later, when I stopped shaking and started crying, I would want people. Not now. I walked away from them down the echoing aisle of the south choir transept. In the gloom I thought I saw a cowled figure preceding me, but when I got to the door no one was there.

I opened the door on much more light than I had expected, and stepped out into a world transformed. From the heavy clouds snow was falling at last, thick, white, beautiful snow, blanketing, softening, cleansing. At the gate I turned back. The cathedral, huge, gray, and serene, brooded on its smooth white cloud and folded its protective wings over Sherebury.

∽20∾

"...SO THAT'S REALLY all the news from here. No one can say it hasn't been an *eventful* Christmas! Love, Dorothy."

That was nearly all of my Christmas correspondence done, thank goodness. It had been tedious writing a slightly different version of murder and mayhem to all the friends and relations, but the thought of mass-producing a "Christmas letter" made me quail. Not that I mind them, but I could *not* see beginning one with, "Well, the holidays are over and all our murders are solved. . . ."

The doorbell rang; Emmy stirred and stretched and went back to sleep.

"Alan, come in. The rest will be along shortly, I expect."

He tossed his hat and coat onto the chair in the hall and went into the parlor. "How's the mistress of the house?" he asked, nodding at the heap of gray fur.

"Back to her usual form and ruling with an iron paw. I spoiled her the first few days she got home, and she's still taking full advantage of my sympathy."

I excused myself to put the kettle on, and by the time I got back to the parlor the rest of my guests had arrived.

"Everybody knows everybody, of course, except Nigel, have you met Dr. Temple?"

Nigel stood up and extended his hand, his manners very much to the fore. "I've heard of you, of course, sir. You're a legend at the university."

Dr. Temple twinkled, his white hair flying away. "And I've heard of you, too, young man."

"Oh, dear," said Inga demurely. "That sounds frightfully ominous."

Jane grunted contentedly.

"Now, Alan," I said when everyone had tea and goodies, "there's one thing I still can't understand. Why was the canon so secretive about the manuscript? A find like that, you'd think he'd have shouted it from the rooftops."

"That's an easy one. He stole it."

"But—who from?" I asked, my grammar deserting me.

"From Greece. He found it, probably when he was involved in that earthquake in Corinth, although we'll never know for certain, of course. But finders aren't keepers in this case. Antiquities belong to the country where they are found, so he stole it from the Greek government."

"Not only that," said Nigel, dripping with youthful scorn, "he took it away from the site, and everyone knows something like that should be left *in situ* until it can be dated, matched up with other artifacts in the same place—all that. One would've thought him a better scholar."

"I reckon it was just too much for him," put in Dr. Temple. "Every researcher dreams of turning up a big discovery, and this one was beyond the wildest dream."

"What do you think he meant to do with it?" asked Inga. "Stolen, and all—he'd scarcely have been able to publish his findings."

Jane snorted. "Doubt he knew himself. Might've taken it back and replanted it and then 'discovered' it again. Probably stole the thing on impulse and then, when he knew what he had . . ."

"Do you think," I asked the room at large, "it was really . . . ?" I couldn't say it. I kept thinking of those shreds of papyrus floating to the cathedral floor.

"Never know," said Jane gruffly. "Sending the remains to the BM for dating, but that's all they can tell. Now."

There was a sober pause.

"Three people died for it," I said finally. "All because George wanted his academic chair, his justification for existence, badly enough to kill. In a way, I hope it was worth it."

"I wonder what Mrs. Chambers is going to do," said Inga, changing the subject.

"So do I," I put in. "I can hardly call on her, or write, but I do feel sorry for her."

"Needn't," said Jane. "Going to sell her house and buy that Victorian ruin out Dilham way. Restore it to glory."

"I thought she liked new houses!"

"George did. Funny woman, Alice. Loyal to him through thick and thin, but never cared much. Too soon to say so, but better off without him."

Emmy smelled the turkey in the sandwiches just then and came over to help herself. When we had chased her away (sandwich in mouth), Dr. Temple grinned mischievously at me.

"What you need, my dear, is another cat."

"Heaven help me! You're surely not trying to find a new home for Soo and Ling?"

"No, indeed, they'd not allow it for a moment! No, but Ling finds herself in a delicate condition. I'm sure a half-Siamese kitten would be just the companion for Esmeralda. Probably her half-sibling, as well." He looked fixedly at Inga, who groaned.

"Mum and Dad really *are* going to have to have Max altered. We'll be settling paternity suits all over town at this rate."

Alan stayed after the party to help me wash the dishes.

"Dorothy," he said as he was leaving, "there's a new Indian restaurant just opened on the High Street. Do you like Indian food?"

"Very much."

"Then let's try it out, shall we? Tomorrow night?"

"I'd enjoy that."

I closed the door and went back to my desk to write the very last Christmas-card reply.

"Dear Bob and Sophie, I appreciate your efforts in looking for a new house for me, but I think I'm going to stay in England, at least for now. Sherebury suits me. . . ."

↭ ECCLESIASTICAL NOTES ↭

FOR THOSE UNFAMILIAR with Church of England architecture and liturgy, I offer the following guide.

"THE CATHEDRAL CHURCH of St. Peter and St. Paul at Sherebury is, like most medieval cathedrals, built on a cruciform (cross-shaped) plan, with the high altar toward the east end. The building is surrounded by a large grassy area known as the "Close" (pronounced with a soft *s*), with an ancient cemetery in one corner and the homes and offices of the dean, bishop, and other cathedral personnel around the edges. One usually enters the cathedral not through the huge west door, which is opened only for ceremonial purposes, but through a smaller door in the south tower, leading into the *south porch*,* and thence into the church. The main body of the church is the *nave*, from the Latin for ship, so-named because it looks, with its curved, ribbed roof, a little like an overturned hull. The nave is flanked by *aisles* on either side, lined with tombs and memorial plaques in the walls and on the floor.

*Italicized terms will be found in the floor plan.

At the east end of the nave there is a *parish altar* at the *crossing*, where the two *transepts* stretch out to north and south. The transepts are also thickly cluttered with tombs and memorials; against the east walls are a number of small chapels, many of them *chantries* endowed centuries ago by the wealthy for the purpose of having masses sung there forever for the repose of their souls. As the years changed religious and political thought, the chantries were stripped of their reason for being, but remain as tiny architectural gems within the larger church.

Sherebury, originally built as an abbey church, has a *chapter house*, where the daily business of the monastery used to be transacted, now used as the cathedral library, and also a *choir screen*, a thick, elaborately carved wall separating the nave, where the laity worshiped at the parish altar, from the *choir*, where the cloistered monks sang their many daily services. The choir screen has a wide, arched doorway through which processions pass and the activity at the *high altar* can be seen from the nave. Most services at Sherebury Cathedral are now held in the choir; the singers—also referred to as the choir (which can be confusing)—and clergy occupy about a third of the *stalls*, or carved oak seats designed for the monks, and the congregation the rest. The choir is also the location of the *cathedra*, the bishop's throne that gives the building its name and its function as the principal church of the diocese. A second set of shorter transepts extends from the choir at the west end of the *chancel*. The south choir transept is the only remaining part of the original abbey church of the eleventh century. The rest burned down in the 1400s and was rebuilt in Perpendicular style. The transept would probably have been torn down and rebuilt next, but Henry VIII's dissolution of the abbeys intervened.

The *apse* is distinguished by marvelous stained-glass windows, by far the best in the cathedral. These are unfortunately invisible from most of the church, since someone in the eighteenth century erected an imposing set of organ pipes on top of the choir screen and completely blocked the view.

Within the Church of England there are various "parties," or sets of liturgical and doctrinal preferences. Sherebury's bishop and dean are both of high church persuasion. This means that their services tend to be very formal and traditional, and to emphasize the similarities with the Roman Catholic Church rather than the differences. Thus the clergy wear full sets of vestments for services, most of the service is sung or chanted instead of being spoken, incense is used for important occasions, genuflections and signs of the cross are made at appropriate moments, and so on. It also follows that the most important service on a Sunday is the Eucharist (or Holy Communion, or Mass), at which bread and wine are consecrated and distributed to the faithful as the Body and Blood of Christ. There are four services at Sherebury every Sunday: an early spoken Eucharist, followed by Matins (Morning Prayer) at which the full glories of the male choir are put to use, followed a little later by a sung Eucharist, the principal service, and, in the late afternoon, Evensong (Evening Prayer), a particularly lovely choral service. Matins and Evensong are said or sung every weekday, as well; there is a spoken Eucharist every morning and a sung one on saints' days and special holy days.

The accompanying floor plan may be of help, particularly to the reader who has never been so fortunate as to visit an English cathedral. For him, or her, I would recommend beginning with Lincoln Cathedral, which really is, in this writer's opinion, the most beautiful church in the world—not counting Sherebury, which, though truly magnificent, exists, alas, only in our imagination.

The town of Sherebury is also fictional, though owing

much to various real places. It is located somewhere in the southeast of England. The Wicked Lady and the Old Bakehouse do exist, but nowhere near Maidstone. I haven't presumed to alter London geography or landscape.

CRACK DOWN
Val McDermid

A Gold Dagger
Winning Writer

"One of my favorite authors."
—*Sara Paretsky*

"Kate Brannigan is a cheeky addition to the growing sisterhood of crime."
—*THE WASHINGTON POST*

Manchester PI Kate Brannigan asks her rock-journalist boyfriend to help her on a case and he ends up behind bars.

Look for CLEAN BREAK coming November 1996